TRAPPED

MICHAEL NORTHROP

www.atombooks.net

ATOM

First published in the United States in 2011 by Scholastic Press
First published in Great Britain in 2011 by Atom

Copyright © 2011 by Michael Northrop

The moral right of the author has been asserted.

A CIP catalogue record for this book
is available from the British Library.

ISBN 978-1-907411-36-6

Printed and bound in Great Britain by
Clays Ltd, St Ives plc

Papers used by Atom are from well-managed forests
and other responsible sources.

MIX
Paper from
responsible sources
FSC
www.fsc.org   FSC® C104740

Atom
An imprint of
Little, Brown Book Group
100 Victoria Embankment
London EC4Y 0DY

An Hachette UK Company
www.hachette.co.uk

www.atombooks.net

For my mom, Sally Ongley Northrop,
who always let us play in the snow
a little too long, which is to say,
just the right amount.

ONE

We were the last seven kids waiting around to get picked up from Tattawa Regional High School. It sounds like an everyday thing, but this wasn't an ordinary day. It was one of those bull's-eyes in history, one of those points where everything comes together, where, if you were at that place at that time, you were part of something big. It meant that we weren't going to get picked up, not on that day and maybe not ever.

It was the day the blizzard started, and it didn't stop for nearly a week. No one had seen anything like it. It was a natural disaster in the way that earthquakes and tidal waves are natural disasters. It wasn't a storm; it was whatever comes after that.

The power lines came down, and the airports closed. The snow was so strong that it seemed to hit the ground in drifts. The roads shut down completely. The plows ground to a halt and stranded themselves, overmatched up front and the snow behind already too deep for them to back up. Really, if you want one quick indicator of what kind of storm it was: Drivers froze in their snowplows.

People hunkered down in their homes. They were used to doing that in this part of New England, but in the past it had always been for six hours, or twelve, or maybe a day at most. This was different, and it required a different kind of waiting. You can hear the details in a thousand coffee shops, at the back table where the locals hang out.

I'll just tell you, though. The nor'easter moved up the coast and stalled, but instead of weakening, it got stronger. From what I heard, it just kind of got wedged there, in between a huge cold front coming down and a massive warm front moving up, scooping up moisture over the Atlantic and dropping it as snow back on land. They still show the picture on TV sometimes: a giant white pinwheel spanning three states.

Inside the homes and shelters, people waited and watched and counted and recounted their canned food. They all asked themselves the same question: How much longer can this last? But they asked it day after day, in lamplight and then candlelight and then in darkness and creeping cold. But that was later on.

4

At the beginning, it was just us, looking out the window and watching the snow fall.

Mr. Gossell stayed with us. He was a gruff guy, a history teacher and assistant football coach. Your school probably has one of those. He sort of carried himself like he was in the army and, I don't know, maybe he had been. He was the last teacher left, but when he shouldered the door open and headed out to get help, well, that was the last we saw of him. We added his name to the list of people we were waiting for.

We imagined headlights cutting through the snow, there to battle the roads and take us home. The driver would throw open the passenger-side door. "Climb aboard," he'd shout. "Hop in! We'll get ya home!"

But we weren't going anywhere. The headlights didn't show. Mr. Gossell, Jason's dad, Krista's mom, whoever it was we were waiting for, they had nothing to do with us anymore. No one did. It was just the seven of us, the seven of us and the endless snow.

TWO

It began falling in the morning. I noticed it at the start of second period, biology, but I guess it could've started at the end of first period. Snow isn't really bound by a class schedule. There wasn't much to it at first, and it'd been snowing a lot that month, so I didn't give it much thought. It was those small flakes, like grains of sugar. By third period, the flakes had fattened up and gotten serious, and people were starting to talk about it.

"Think they'll let us out early?" Pete said as we gathered our stuff and headed for Spanish.

I looked out the window and sized it up. It was really coming down and there was already an inch or two on the sill.

"Could be," I said. "Is it supposed to be a big one?"

"Supposed to be huge: 'Winter Storm Warning,'" he said. "Where you been?"

"School, practice, homework, whatever. Excuse me for not watching the frickin' Weather Channel."

"Yeah, well, you might want to check it out sometime," he said. "Then you wouldn't be wearing Chucks in a nor'easter."

I looked down at my sneakers. "Well, if it's as big as all that, they'll probably let us go."

"I hope you're right, Weems," he said.

My name is Scotty Weems. I prefer Scotty, but most people, even my friends, call me Weems. I guess it's easy to say, and maybe some people think it's funny. It doesn't bother me that much. I'm just glad that Snotty Streams never really caught on as a nickname.

Anyway, I'm an athlete, so I made peace with my last name a long time ago. Since I was a little kid in T-ball, I heard it shouted every time I did something right and every time I screwed up, too. These days it's on the back of my basketball jersey. I like to think that someday people will be chanting it from the bleachers: "Weems! Weems! Weems!" Chanting fans make any name sound good.

Anyway, that's me. I'll be sort of like your guide through

all of this. Some of the others might've seen things differently, and some of them might've told it better, but you don't get to pick. You don't because, for one thing, not all of us made it.

It was a Tuesday, and before the sky started falling the main thing on my radar was the start of hoops season. The first game was supposed to be that night, home against Canterbridge. So when Pete said "Think they'll let us out early?" what I heard was "Think they'll cancel the game?" So we had different feelings on the subject right from the get-go.

Pete Dubois was one of my best friends, him and Jason Gillispie. The three of us were pretty tight. Pete was just, like, a normal kid. It was sort of his role. It might sound strange, being known for what you aren't, but Pete wasn't a jock or a Future Farmer of America or a student council member, and he wasn't super hip or incredibly smart. He was just a normal sophomore. He listened to standard-issue rock music and wore whatever clothes he'd been given for Christmas or his birthday. You needed some kids like that, otherwise all you had were competing factions of freaks, all dressed in outfits that amounted to uniforms and trying to play their music louder than yours.

So for Pete, early dismissal just meant more time at home, playing video games and eating pizza rolls. For me, it meant not collecting the payoff for all those hours of practice I'd put in over the off-season, all those jump shots I'd taken in the gym and out in the driveway and at the courts down behind the library. It meant time for the other shooting guards to catch up, to keep their minutes, or to take some of mine.

"They're going to cancel the game," I said to Pete. "That's for sure."

"Oh, yeah," said Pete. "Bummer."

Pete didn't shoot hoops, not on the team anyway. Neither did Jason. They were the same friends I'd always had, the neighborhood kids I'd ridden bikes with in the cemetery when we were like nine. Our moms sent us there because it was better to ride around where everyone else was dead than out on the road where the traffic would kill you.

I guess it's kind of weird to still have the same friends as when you were a little kid. It's not like you're expected to move on by high school, but you're definitely allowed. And most jocks run in packs, you know? But I was a sophomore on varsity, so I was kind of an outsider on the team anyway. There were only a few of us, and I wasn't a star like Kyle or buried deep on the bench like Joey.

So I was an outside shooter and just kind of outside in general. I didn't need to hang out with my teammates, though. Those guys would like me just fine when I was a starter, and that was my goal for this season. As for my real friends—Pete, Jason, and maybe Eric on his good days—I didn't have to prove anything to them. I didn't have to shoot 40 percent from downtown for them; I didn't have to shoot at all.

"I'll tell you one thing," said Pete as we settled into our seats across the aisle from each other in Spanish. "This better not get in the way of the dance on Friday, 'cause I am going to get me some."

"Yeah, some of your own right hand afterwards," I said, because you can't concede a point like that.

"No way, man," he said, and he wanted to say something more, something about how Marissa was going to be there and had I already forgotten that he'd gotten his hands up her shirt just last week? And if he did ask that, I would say, "How could I, as many times as you've reminded all of us about it since then?" But the bell rang and cut him off.

"*Hola,* class," said Ms. Chaney in her signature fractured Spanish.

"*Hola,* Señora Chaney," said the girls, mostly, some of them burying their noses deeper by rolling their *r*'s.

I looked over at Pete, and he gave me that look, opening his eyes wide and shrugging his shoulders forward as if to say, "You know what I mean?" I did, but that dance would never happen. Looking back on all of this, I shiver a little, thinking of what took its place. Images creep in: black smoke and blue skin.

But again, I'm getting ahead of myself, way ahead. You haven't even met everybody yet. We caught up with Jason after class. Everyone was talking about the snow. It was coming down in rolling sheets by then, like white curtains blowing in the wind. But Jason wanted to talk about his ridiculous *Flammenwerfer,* which was kind of like his pet project.

The *Flammenwerfer* was a go-kart, or was going to be. Jason was attempting to piece it together in shop class. He'd spent the entire marking period working on it, and if it didn't work, he was straight-up going to fail. Plus, he insisted it was going to be sweet. If he finished it, if it worked, if, if, if.

"Come on, guys. We'll have the place to ourselves," he was saying.

He meant that we could screw around with the power tools and maybe mess around with some of the stuff the other kids had brought in for their own projects.

Flammenwerfer was the German word for *flamethrower*. I only knew that because Jason told me. I didn't speak German; I was having enough trouble with Spanish. But he'd told me, and everyone else he knew, and more than once. Now, when you think German weapons, you think World War II. You think the Big One and all those movies you've seen. That tells you something about Jason, not that he's a Nazi or anything, but that he's always been kind of fascinated with wars and military stuff.

Now, obsessed with army guys is one thing at age ten—I mean, we all were—but at fifteen? It's maybe a little bit of a warning sign, you know? Jason kind of freaked some people out, not the kids as much as some of the teachers. Truth is, he'd probably freak me out a little too, if I hadn't known him since we were really little.

Case in point: He was wearing a long-sleeve blue T-shirt that said, "Long distance, the next best thing to being there." It was an old phone company slogan, I think, but the picture on the shirt was of a sniper's rifle.

"Can't do it, man," I told him. "I've got a game tonight."

No one responded for a second or two, and they managed not to laugh or roll their eyes, but I knew what they were thinking. "Maybe," I added. I was surprised how defensive I sounded, and I guess that was enough to get a reply.

"No way that's gonna happen," said Jason, flicking his hand

14

toward the window and the snow outside. Without even looking out there I knew he was right, but it still kind of ticked me off, that hand flick. It seemed like he was just dismissing it. It's the first game of the season, I was thinking. You can't just wave it off like you're shooing away a fly.

"Come on, guys," said Jason. "It's almost done. I'll be able to test the engine again soon."

"Yeah," said Pete, "and then you just have to figure out some new way to keep that engine hooked up to the frickin' wheels. If it even works."

"Whoa, whoa, whoa . . . What is this negativity?" said Jason, sort of fake-offended. "Not if, when. When it works."

"When it explodes, more like," I said.

"Well," said Jason, breaking into a smile, "at least that'll be cool to watch."

"Yeah, I don't need all these fingers anyway," I said.

We were just joking around at this point, and that meant, basically, that we were going to do it. We couldn't bust on him and then leave him hanging. It's hard to explain why not— I guess because that would be one thing too many. We all knew we were probably going to stay after and help him, but there were still some logistics to work out, some possible defenses.

"I don't think so, man," I said. "If it's early dismissal, there won't be any late buses."

"Nah, it's cool. My dad'll pick us up. He's got the truck— four-wheel drive, you know?—and he's working like two miles from here today, just across the river in Canton."

The high school was kind of out in the middle of nowhere, on a big tract of what used to be farmland. That's kind of a big deal, and I'll get back to it later. For now, all you need to know is that two miles away was about as close as anyone was liable to be.

"I don't want to be here all night," said Pete.

"They knock off at like four, at the latest."

"Yeah," I said, just going through the motions of resistance at this point, "but will shop even be open? Holloway'll be gone just like everyone else."

"Are you kidding, man? He loves it when anyone stays after."

That was true. The old man enjoyed any sign that people were taking an interest in his class. Jason paused and then said, "Lock up when you leave," in a pretty good imitation of Holloway's voice.

I looked over at Pete. He shrugged. As lame as Jason's junker of a would-be go-kart was, it wasn't like Pete and I had a ton of exciting projects of our own to work on. My game wasn't going to happen, and it was just another Tuesday for Pete.

"Alright," I said at last, "but let's at least wait for the announcements."

We knew they were coming: Game canceled would probably be first, then early dismissal. A speaker hung on the wall above our heads in the hallway. But it stayed silent for now, and we had to bust our butts to get to class.

THREE

The next class started, and I think it's fair to say no one was in the mood for geometry. I don't even think Mr. Peragrino was, and as near as anyone could tell, he lived for that stuff. He gave us a pop quiz anyway. He had it printed up already, and I guess he felt like it was as good a way to wait for the announcement as any.

As soon as we all had our heads bent down over the quiz, cell phones started going off. Not ringing, of course. Cell phones weren't allowed at Tattawa, and they were kind of not kidding about that. The first time you were caught, you got a warning, and after that you took "the suspension bridge." That meant detention the second time, a longer detention the third time, and then suspension.

I was more concerned about indirect proofs at the moment, but the room was quiet and every now and then you could hear a cell vibrating in someone's backpack, like a big, fist-sized bug trying to get out. Kids would cough or scrutch their chairs back to cover it up, but let's be honest—if you're smart enough to teach indirect proofs, you're smart enough to figure that out.

Peragrino didn't move, though, didn't even say anything. He should've been adding names to the list left and right, but I think he understood: Parents were getting worried, wondering if their little angels (Ha!) were coming home soon. And, I mean, isn't that what cell phones were for, like, originally, before all the apps and web surfing and rapping ringtones? When I was a little kid, I had a dinky round cell phone with one button so that I could call my mom or she could call me. It had some embarrassing name, like Doodlebug, but it really should've been called Leash.

Finally, fifteen minutes and four-and-a-half questions later, not counting one that I skipped, the loudspeaker crackled to life with the official word. "May I have your attention for an announcement, please? This is your principal speaking," it began. I don't know why. I mean, we obviously knew it was Throckmarten, and he obviously had our attention. "Due to worsening conditions, school will be dismissed at one o'clock this afternoon. All athletic and extracurricular activities have been canceled. All buses leave at one fifteen. Thank you."

Pete leaned across the aisle and high-fived a kid named John, who everyone called Drumstick. Of course, Drumstick was going home at one fifteen, and Pete would be stuck here with Jason and me till four or so.

Drumstick turned to high-five me. At first, I was going to leave him hanging. I mean, my game had just been canceled. I hesitated maybe half a beat and then reached out and slapped his hand anyway. When it came right down to it, it wasn't about my game or whether I'd be on the first bus out. We were forced to go to high school, stuck in here and marched around like livestock. Anytime they had to let us loose, it was sort of like a victory, you know? We knew it didn't amount to much, but we broke off little bits of freedom, and we high-fived when we did.

The kids whose phones had gone off before took the opportunity to stick their hands deep down into their backpacks and bags to switch them off. They didn't really need to: The lines were already getting swamped and the service getting worse with the weather, but none of us realized that yet. I didn't have to worry about it, in any case: I didn't have mine with me. I'd already had my warning this marking period, and detention was not an option for me because it meant missing practice.

"Alright, cool it," said Mr. Peragrino. "This class is not over yet."

And that was true enough. It seemed a little unfair that we would have to finish this quiz after all—I really had no clue about question three—but after that, all we had was lunch, so we were basically done. I mean, the way it was coming down now, they probably would've sent us home on the spot, except I think they were legally obligated to feed us before throwing us out into the snow.

Since it would turn out to be my last real meal for quite a while—if you can call the school lunches at Tattawa a real meal—I guess I should've been grateful. I actually remember little things about that lunch, like how the whole cafeteria had a bursting-through-the-roof sort of energy to it. It was louder than usual and people were moving between the tables, talking and laughing.

I remember the snow, drifting sideways into half crescents in the windowpanes, and I remember that I didn't eat my corn. I don't know if I took a bite and thought it was a little too soggy or if I just remembered that it had been soggy the last time, but I left it there on my tray.

As dumb as this sounds, that bothered me for days. I mean, soggy or not, it was decent corn prepared by people who were at least borderline professionals. It was definitely a whole lot better than what I'd end up eating soon enough, and I'd just thrown it away. I still remember the little flash of yellow as I pushed the tray onto the conveyor belt that took it into the back of the kitchen, where the giant, hissing dishwashing machines were. Whoever thought you could be haunted by corn niblets?

After lunch, Pete, Jason, and I sat on the floor of the hallway outside the library and watched the buses roll slowly into the storm. The hallway had these big, tall safety glass windows. Sitting there, looking forward, it provided a pretty amazing view of the snow outside.

Mr. Trever, the assistant principal, hustled by and stopped short. He was a big black dude, which I only mention because, generally speaking, this area had about as much color as this snowstorm. "What are you guys still doing here?" he said.

We had to sort of crane our necks to look up at him. "Jason's dad is picking us up," I said. "He's got the 4x4."

Trever considered this for a second, or, more likely, he considered us for a second. We weren't really troublemakers, but none of us were going to be elected Student of the Year, either. We were sort of right in the middle, discipline-wise. I'm sure that made us the hardest sort of kid for Trever to figure out.

"A four-wheel drive, huh?" he said, still trying to size us up.

"Yeah," said Jason. "You know, these big buses on these slick roads . . . Just seems like the truck's a little safer. Plus, he's just down the road, working in Canton today."

I looked over at Jason. He sounded pretty convincing. He was doing this right because everything he said was true, he was just leaving something out. Those were the easiest lies to tell.

Trever didn't say anything for a second. He was thinking about something, maybe about how the school buses could barely make it up some of the hills around here, even in the best weather.

What Jason was leaving out, of course, was that his dad wasn't planning on picking us up for another several hours. At this rate, I estimated, that could amount to another foot of snow. (I wasn't thinking big enough, of course; it was more like three times that.) But if Jason wasn't saying, Trever wasn't asking. In the end, he didn't let us stay because he trusted us. He let us stay because he drove a two-door Toyota. It was like one step up from a bike, and he wanted to get home sooner rather than later.

"Alright," he said, "but go wait by the gymnasium with Gossell. He's in charge of pickups, and they'll be locking all of these other doors in a few minutes anyway."

We sat there, our heads tilted up at him.

"Now," he said, and we climbed to our feet.

FOUR

When Trever turned right to head to the faculty parking lot, we knew enough to turn left, as if we were heading for the gym and Mr. Gossell. Once we couldn't hear his footsteps anymore, we doubled back and headed for shop or, as the plaque on the door read, the INDUSTRIAL ARTS ROOM.

The door was locked, though. The plaque might as well have said, CLOSED FOR SEASON.

"Uh, moron," I said, rattling the handle one more time and turning toward Jason. "You did clear this with Holloway, right?"

"Uh, he said he'd still be here. He said just to stop by."

"Was this before or after the announcement?"

"Um, before, I guess," said Jason. "I just sort of assumed he knew we'd get out early. I mean, everyone knew."

"Dude," I said. "Holloway is, like, one thousand years old. Seriously. Who knows what he knows anymore?"

"Yeah," said Jason, kicking the base of the wall with the toe of his boot. "Fair point."

Pete put his face up against the window on the door. "Wait a sec," he said. "There's something moving in there."

"Something?" I said. "What is it, a puma?"

"Someone, I mean. Also, shut up."

Pete put his hand up above his eyes to shield them, like he was gazing off into a sunset. "It's Holloway."

"Told you," said Jason.

"You're still a moron," I said.

"Shut up, Weems," he said. "I aren't not no moron."

Now we could hear Holloway moving around, his heavy footsteps getting closer to the door. We all sort of stepped back, even though the door opened inward. The shop teacher appeared in the hallway wearing an enormous parka and gigantic snowmobile boots. Holloway had been put on this planet nearly a century earlier and had aged none too gracefully into the sort of old-timer who took winter seriously.

He was the kind of guy who would sit around in the coffee shop behind the pharmacy talking about the "Blizzard of '93." I know, because I'd seen him back there, nursing his coffee with the other old-timers and alternating between their two conversational options: complaining about the present or reminiscing about the past.

At least once I overheard him saying "the mother of all blizzards." From the way he was dressed, it looked like he might've been the only one who knew that the mother of that one had just blown into town. The hood of his parka, lined with fake gray fur and looking like roadkill, drooped down behind his head. He looked around at the three of us and then stomped his huge black boots twice—*Pdhump! Pdhump!*—like an animal sending a warning. I guess he was just pressing his feet in all the way.

"I don't know, boys," he said. "I think maybe you should be getting on home."

"Uh," said Jason, by which he meant, "You said it would be OK when I asked you this morning."

Holloway was unmoved by the eloquence of Jason's argument, and I knew there was a war going on in his head. There were two things he really valued. The first was shop class. He was always downright delighted when any of us asked to stay after and put in some extra time. His old face would just crack open with joy, with deep lines spreading the length of it. It kind of made you smile, just to see an old man so happy.

He'd probably been doing this for half a century, but time was sort of running against him. A lot of high schools didn't even have shop class anymore, and most kids were angling to get something more out of their lives than tuning up cars or fixing refrigerators. These days, students—even students in

Podunk towns like ours—were supposed to be part of the Information Age or the Post-Industrial Workforce or some other thing that didn't involve power tools.

And, I mean, it was kind of dicey, leaving kids unsupervised in a room full of edges and motors and blades. But that wasn't really part of Holloway's thinking—he thought of hacksaws and blowtorches the way that other teachers thought of pencils or calculators—and we'd already signed our lives away anyway, our lives and our limbs. Every kid who took shop had to fill out a "legal disclaimer" form that "absolved the school" of responsibility for "accidental death or dismemberment" due to everything up to and including "gross incompetence" and "faulty equipment." Looking around at the decades-old tools and the Old Man Time teacher, the forms had been a big joke when they were handed out at the start of the year. They'd been an enormous laugh. We were fifteen. We considered ourselves invulnerable and had yet to be proven wrong.

It wasn't the creaky tools that were worrying Holloway, though. It was the snow. That was the other thing he really valued: Like a lot of New Englanders who've reached a certain age and haven't had the common sense to leave, he really had a thing for winter, like it was some beautiful beast that had to be respected. It was part of that whole hardship-equals-character thing. Oldsters loved that, the idea that character was something you could accumulate over time.

"Really coming down out there, boys," he said, looking over his shoulder at the windows against the far wall. He put his hand on the door as he did this, and it seemed like the old guy was going to lock us out.

Jason saw it too and managed to string together a few actual sentences this time, telling Holloway about his dad and the 4x4. "And besides," Jason tagged on at the end, "the buses just left."

"You're all from Cambria, right?" Holloway said.

And we were. Tattawa Regional High School was made up of students from three towns — Soudley, Little River, and North Cambria — but the three of us were all from North Cambria. And since I'd seen him in the coffee shop, so was Holloway. He was considering driving us home himself.

"My dad is seriously just down the road," said Jason, "and he's got to come this way anyhow."

Holloway looked at him, not impressed.

"Plus, it will only be about half an hour," said Jason, lying. "Forty-five minutes, tops."

"Hardly seems worth it," said Holloway.

"Yeah, I guess my dad was real concerned about the storm, too."

I felt a little bad listening to Jason lay it on so thick and having to nod along with my eyes wide open in that he's-telling-the-truth way. It was just the right line, though, and Holloway took his hand off the door handle.

"Band saw's locked up," he said by way of good-bye. "Torch is almost out of gas."

Once we were inside, we closed the door behind us and threw off our coats.

"Cold in here," said Pete.

There was a small pile of snow under one of the windows, just starting to melt.

"I guess he wanted a closer look," I said.

"At what?"

And Pete was right. You couldn't see anything out the windows. The view was an unbroken sheet of white. It was jarring but also a little misleading, because these windows were in the back of the school, and the school was built on a sort of hillside. The back of the gym was off to our right, but on this side of the school, the ground just fell away, down to where the playing fields were and the river beyond that. So standing here and looking out these windows, we were really just looking at open sky and some hills off in the distance. Except that we couldn't see those hills anymore. It was like the snow had erased them, or buried them. All that was left was a softly shifting whiteness.

"Man," said Jason. "Look at that."

Look at it? I thought. We're frickin' stuck in it. I knew right then that we'd made a mistake. It's like sometimes you're so intent on talking your way in that you don't really think about whether or not you want to be there.

"Maybe your dad should come a little early?" I said to Jason.

He looked back toward the door, as if Holloway might still be hanging around watching us. Then he dug down into his pocket and pulled out his cell. "Probably," he said, "but I can't get through."

"Not at all?" I said.

He glanced at the screen again, barely looking, just confirming what he already knew. He shrugged. "I had, like, one bar earlier, but I don't think they get jack-squat out there, and now I don't have anything. At all. Like zero-point-zero bars."

"What about you?" I said to Pete.

He looked back at the door too.

"Would you two stop that? Holloway left like a rocket. He probably ran right out of those boots."

Pete took his phone out. It was more for video games, and the screen flashed on with a little burst of colors.

"Nah," he said. "No bars for the phone, and I can never get online out here anyway. Text I sent home, like, an hour ago is still sitting there waiting for a signal."

"Man," I said, looking out the window. This high school was always a one-bar wonderland, and even a light rain made it worse. I thought about the handful of phones going off in geometry, but it was definitely coming down much heavier now. "Guess it's the snow?"

"Or everyone trying to call at once," said Jason.

"Or both," said Pete.

"That blows," I said. It was like an unintentional joke, but I don't think anyone noticed. We all just stood there, looking out the window. The snow couldn't possibly keep up like this, I thought. No way, right? And there wasn't much we could do about it now. I mean, it's like, raise your hand if you're God, right? Jason's dad would be here in a few hours. Or he wouldn't. Nothing else to do; time to work on a crappy go-kart.

FIVE

An hour in, we were leaning over the metal framework of the chassis. Jason had the circular grinder and we were all wearing safety goggles. They were uncomfortable and wearing them might seem like a lame thing to do with no teacher around, but I sort of like having a matching set of eyes, you know? I just enjoy the whole being-able-to-see-and-not-being-deformed thing. There was a kid here last year with a messed-up eye. Now he was in juvie. It was a whole big thing.

Anyway, I was leaning in and waiting for the moment when Jason would go too far grinding off the rust and old paint and would put a hole in the tubing, so then I could call him a moron again. But before he did, we heard this clacking, banging sound that had nothing to do with the metal tubing or the circular grinder or anything else we were doing. Someone was at the door, rattling the handle. Jason stopped grinding and we all shifted the goggles up onto our foreheads.

"Whoozat?" said Pete, looking over at us. The outline of his goggles was still stamped into the skin around his eyes. He looked ridiculous, but I guess I did too.

"One way to find out. It's not exactly a secret we're here," I said, the noise of the circular grinder still ringing in my ears.

"Aw, man," said Pete. "I told you we shouldn't've busted that thing out."

"What?" said Jason. "I've got to grind it down before we can repaint it."

"Before *you* can repaint it," I said.

"Whatever; we'll just tell 'em Holloway said it was OK," said Jason.

We were all thinking the same thing. We figured it was Trever or someone like that at the door, and we were going to be in hot water for staying after in a full-bore blizzard and using power tools unsupervised. It seemed like we could probably get slammed for either of those things and that both of them together could add up to some real trouble. Again, we weren't the kind of kids who went around chasing gold stars, but we weren't the kind who thought detention was a badge of honor either.

And like I said before: I'd miss practice. That would suck and I'd be running laps for a week. Coach Kielty was always yelling at me as it was. The assistant coach told me it was because I had "a chance to be something special." But I didn't know that for sure. All I knew was that Coach always seemed to have one-and-a-half of his two eyes on me.

Anyway, it didn't occur to us until we got close to the door that it might be a student out there, and it definitely didn't occur to us that it would be *that* student. From what I'd heard, he barely even qualified as one.

As we got closer to the door, the banging picked up. Whoever was out there was practically shaking the door off its hinges.

"Calm down," I said. "Just chill."

Pete got to the door first.

"Oh, crap," he whispered back to us. "It's Les Goddard."

Les Goddard was bad news, like seriously. His full name was Leslie, apparently. Somewhere in this world, I guess, that's a guy's name, but this wasn't that place. Maybe that's why he was such a thug. He's the kind of guy you just sort of assume is armed in some way. Maybe not with a gun or anything fully criminal like that, but with something improvised, something that a truly mean dude would find and keep, like a box cutter or a razor blade or just a hunk of metal.

Once he saw us, the door went still, and we heard him from the hallway. "Open up, ladies." It came through the thick door at the volume of normal speech, but we knew it hadn't started out that way. The guy was standing out in the hallway, shouting.

"Well," I said, "I guess we should see what he wants."

"Before he puts his hand through the window," said Pete.

We were speaking under our breath, a little more than a whisper, because we were all right by the door now, just a foot or two from the psychopath on the other side of it. I reached out for the handle and turned it.

"Hey, man," I said, my voice deepening in some subconscious bluff. I stepped back as he pushed the door inward.

"Hey, loser," said Les. "Who's in here, just you three?"

"Yep," I said.

Les stepped fully into the room, nodded at Jason, and said, "Hey."

Jason and Les weren't friends, exactly, but Les seemed to give Jason some credit for the whole military thing, the novelty T-shirts and fatigue pants and all that. All the stuff we busted on Jason for, basically. I think Jason—a nice guy who sort of played at being dangerous, if you ask me—found that a little flattering. I mean, Les really was dangerous. He, like, radiated danger.

We all knew him, in any case. He took shop too.

"What are you guys doing here? Early dismissal, you know."

"Working on Jason's stupid kart," I said. I gestured toward the back of the room, where little bits of paint and rust still hung in the air. It occurred to me then, just a random thought that skittered in and out of my brain, that we probably should've been wearing masks to keep that stuff out of our lungs.

Les sniffed the air. Even over here, it smelled of burnt paint. "Yeah," he said. "Heard the grinder."

"What are you still doing here?" said Pete. He sounded friendly, almost casual. I'm sure he had to work hard to get the tone right, but the tone turned out not to matter. Up to this point, Les had been almost friendly to us, but that wasn't his style and he seemed to remember that now.

40

He answered the question with a grunt and a shrug. When his shoulders came back down, nice Les was gone and we were once again looking at the only sophomore the seniors were legitimately scared of. This was a guy who, according to one story, had been suspended for throwing a chair through a window in second grade. Who does something like that in second grade? Who's that frickin' strong? The most trouble I got in at that age involved rubber cement.

Something about Pete's question had triggered the change in Les. I was thinking, what's wrong with asking "What are you still doing here?" And then it occurred to me, and I had to try hard not to laugh out loud. I probably would've been knocked out if I had, but it really was funny.

He wouldn't come right out and say it—it's not the kind of thing you'd admit—but the reason he was still here was that he'd gone to detention. Even though there was none after early dismissal. I mean, of course there wasn't; there were no late buses. He'd probably been going for a week and had gone again out of sheer force of habit.

I kept the smile off my face and looked off to the side.

"How you guys getting home?" he said, his voice cold now.

Long story short, he was looking for a ride. The main problem—apart from the fact that Les was a psycho and none of us exactly wanted to cram in next to him for a long, slow ride through a storm that seemed to get worse every minute—was that Les lived in Soudley. That was a long haul, and Jason told him, as politely and delicately as possible, that there was just no frickin' way. If it had been Pete or me, Les might've killed the messenger, but he accepted it from Jason with nothing more

41

than a few F-bombs. And really, what could he do? It was all true. We lived where we lived, and he lived where he lived. And, man, it was really coming down out there.

"You might, uh," I began. I was wading back into the conversation because I was a little scared of Les—I'll admit that—but I also wanted him gone. And there was one other thing that was true: There were three of us and there was one of him. "You might want to go ask Gossell. He's over by the gym or something. Trever says he's in charge of all that stuff, coordinating the rides or whatever."

"Yeah?" said Les.

"Yeah," I said. "He might be able to hook you up."

We were all quiet for a few moments. Les was standing there, thinking. I shifted my weight from one foot to the other.

"This blows," he said, and left.

We listened to his footsteps fade away down the hallway, and then I reached out and swung the door closed.

"Total psycho," said Pete.

"Yep," I said. It was like you could feel the atmosphere in the room returning to normal, like in a movie after they seal the air lock. "He's right though, it's time to get out of here."

"Wow," said Jason, looking out the window. It was just white out there. It looked like a thick fog, but we knew it wasn't.

"That is not good," I said.

There was a little shuffling around as Pete and Jason checked their cells. Still nothing. Pete's text was still in the UNSENT/PENDING folder, along with a second one from him and a new one from me to my mom.

"Think your dad might show up early anyway?" said Pete.

"Yeah," said Jason. "Can't imagine they're doing much work in all this."

"Maybe we should get over there," I said, "in case he shows up."

"Yeah," said Jason. "In case he shows up early."

In case he shows up at all.

SIX

There was a little circle of people in the hallway outside the gym when we arrived: four kids and one teacher, all standing near the double doors. It looked like a field trip just beginning to assemble. The three of us joined the group, bringing the total to eight. That was the most there would ever be. From here on out, the number would only go down.

I was feeling wired and nervous. Looking out the windows on the walk over, I'd been blown away by the view but also kind of relieved. There was something to look at again, instead of that blank white void we'd been looking at out the back windows of the shop. Out front, there was a wide front lawn and some trees. The lawn was a solid field of white now, and the trees were covered in thick snow. Their limbs were bent under the weight, but at least I could see them. I used them to gauge distances and estimate where the empty parking lot was buried.

The slope beyond the school was just barely visible through the storm, climbing through the slanting snow up toward Route 7. There were no cars on 7, though. There was no movement at all except the steadily falling snow. No cars: That's when I began to understand, and my nerves stretched tighter and tighter as I walked.

The sight of the little cluster of people huddled near the door an hour and a half after the school had shut down didn't help much, apart from making me feel like we weren't in this alone. I thought about my mom again. With my text still backed up on the runway, she had no way to know that I'd stayed after. Even if Pete's phone got enough service to send the thing, there was a decent chance that my mom's wouldn't get it.

I should've tried to call earlier, before it got so bad, even just from the office phone. I guess I didn't see the point. She worked till five, and I was supposed to get picked up at four. Home by four thirty, I figured, but that scenario was looking a little rosy at this point, and she'd be home from work by now. There'd been an ice storm a few weeks earlier, not even all that bad, and they'd sent her whole office home early. She'd definitely be home by now. I just kind of told myself that and turned the page.

The first kid I recognized in the little group was Les. He

wasn't facing us, but we'd just seen him and I knew what he was wearing. He was standing just outside the little circle, as if he was trying to start a new ring but no one had joined him. I could tell from his body language that he hadn't gotten good news, or if he had, he hadn't cared for the way it was delivered. He wasn't slouched and defeated; he was coiled up and tense. He looked like he was going to hit something, maybe the wall.

And there was Gossell — Mr. Gossell, Coach Gossell, whatever — and I wasn't too thrilled to see him, either. He was running his hand through his beard the way he did in history class. He probably thought it made him look more manly or "distinguished" or whatever, but it just made me wonder why anyone would want to grow a beard. There were patches of gray in it that made him look old, probably older than he was, because other than the beard his hair was still dark. I guess once you're old enough for any gray hair at all, there's not much point in trying to minimize the damage.

On the plus side, there were girls. There were two freshman chicks, Krista O'Rea and her best friend, Julie Anders. Or maybe it was Enders. Really, it was hard to concentrate on Julie when Krista was around. It was hard to concentrate on anything.

Krista was wearing a blue wool hat, even though she was indoors: a blue hat and a sweater. She turned around at the sound of our footsteps. She had thick brown hair and her eyes were sort of blue-gray. Her skin had just a few reddish brown freckles here and there. But it wasn't the colors as much as the way it was all arranged. If I could include a picture here, I would.

And did I mention her body? Because I will, repeatedly. She wasn't tall, but she had that awesome combination of just enough curves on a tight, athletic body. Soccer in the fall, hoops in the winter. Really, they shouldn't let girls like her mingle with the general population, not in high school anyway. Half the time the guys here were so stuffed with hormones and frustration that we walked down the hallways stiff-legged and ready to burst.

Her eyes flashed past mine and sort of froze me in place. I read once that an avalanche can move so fast and hard that it will suck the air right out of your lungs. It was like that: one quick look that took the wind right out of me. I didn't actually gasp, but it was only because I'd seen Krista before. Many times. She was on my bus route.

Just that morning, I'd spent about twenty quality minutes staring at the back of her neck on the bus, wordless and possibly drooling. Maybe that sounds creepy. It wasn't active staring, it was more like, I don't know, a trance. In any case, if I'd known she was over here waiting, I wouldn't have spent so much time in shop.

Not that I would've said anything to her. She tied me in knots.

Now she was standing next to Julie, who was turning to say something to her. It was no surprise that they were together. It would've been more surprising to see the two of them apart. They were the kind of best friends who had tons of pictures of each other in their lockers. Still, I wondered what they were doing here after school on a day like this. I wondered if I'd have the guts to ask.

The last member of the little circle, the one standing farthest away from us, was Elijah. His full name was Elijah James. I'd always thought his name would've been less strange the other way around: James Elijah. Not that you even needed a last name with a first name like that. There weren't any other Elijahs around that I knew of. Maybe two hundred years ago there might've been.

He was a weird kid, in any case. He wasn't exactly a goth, but those kids would've loved it if he had been. He was legitimately strange in ways they could only play at. He didn't wear all black and mope around. He wore the same few ratty old sweaters and walked around with these clear, wide-open eyes, like he was seeing things you weren't.

I remember, maybe like mid-September, I was walking along the hallway outside the library, and he was inside. He was always in there. I saw him through one of the long windows that ran along the door. It was just a glimpse. He was balancing a coin on the tip of his pen. The coin—I think it was a quarter—wasn't wobbling. It wasn't moving at all. It was like it was stuck on there, like it was welded. Elijah was just looking at it, balancing it.

He was a sophomore, like Jason, Pete, and me; but he wasn't like Jason, Pete, and me. He was wearing a sweater with alternating bands of brown and tan. It made him look sort of like a giant bleached-out bumblebee, the kind you find when you clean out behind a window screen. It always seemed like maybe someone else had dressed him and he hadn't really noticed what they'd put him in yet. And now he was one of seven kids remaining at Tattawa Regional High School on the first day of the worst blizzard in the history of the continental United States.

SEVEN

We sat there staring out the windows for rides that we weren't sure were coming. There was a pay phone at the end of the hall, just outside the gym, but when I walked over to it right after I arrived, everyone else told me not to bother. It was like this collective murmur: "Lines'r-down-don't-bother-yeah-right."

Right after that, Gossell said, "Might as well take out those cell phones and i-things. I know half of you have one hidden somewhere, and you can consider this hallway your detention anyway."

He was right: just about half. Pete and Jason had theirs; the girls had one iPhone between them (it turned out to be Krista's, but they seemed to have joint custody); and Elijah had an old flip-open, "clamshell" type phone. But mine was sitting on my dresser at home, and Les didn't seem to have anything, either.

Of course, having them was one thing, and using them was another. People tried to call for a while, but then Pete said that texts had a better shot because they were "smaller." I wasn't sure about the science behind that, but I knew you could keep trying to resend a text until it went through.

"If anyone gets through, let me know," Gossell said after a few frustrated attempts of his own. Then he added, not really to anyone in particular, "I volunteered down in New Orleans after Hurricane Katrina. There was no service for weeks. Same thing after . . ."

His voice trailed off and I didn't catch the last word. Some other big disaster, I figured. We'd done a whole thing on Hurricane Katrina in social studies back in junior high: the government response, the cleanup, and all of that. Our social studies teacher at North Cambria was kind of an old hippie, though. It was harder to picture Gossell down there doing that "Rebuild for a Brighter Future" stuff, but, I don't know, maybe he was really religious or something.

Pete was playing a video game and flipping over every time he got killed to check on those same sad, stranded texts. Jason alternated between trying to call and staring out into the snow in the direction his dad would be coming from.

After a while, the dialing and texting trailed off. Everyone basically got the point, turned their ringtones up to max volume, and waited. We were all really keyed up, and there was a weird sense of competition. You could see it in people's eyes, in their quick little side-glances. Would Jason's dad get here in his truck before Krista's mom got here in her Subaru? Would either of them get here before whatever was coming to pick up Elijah, a hearse maybe? And would anyone end up giving Les a ride?

I was feeling it too. It's not like I had anything against the others, but I didn't want to be left behind. It was sort of good to know that Jason, Pete, and I were all waiting for the same guy, because it meant that I wouldn't be the last one here.

I guess that feeling of not being alone was important to everyone. We had the whole hallway to wait in, and we probably could've strayed a lot farther than that. Gossell was supervising us, but he didn't give the impression of caring much. He had his own problems, I guess. We probably could've gone back to the shop, for all he cared, but we didn't. No one went anywhere. We waited in a cluster of warm bodies, just off to the side of the main door.

Sometimes we talked, but it was quiet in the hall and the sound sort of echoed. It made you a little self-conscious. Like, I said a few dumb things to Pete — I was talking just to talk, you know? — but everyone could hear it. They were probably thinking "Well, that was a dumb thing to say" or "Who cares?" And they weren't wrong. You could whisper, but that just called more attention to it. That's when people couldn't help but listen.

So the talk would flare up and die down, flare up and die down, but nothing much got said and the quiet spells in between got longer and longer. We just sat and waited, looking out the windows for our opportunity to get out, looking out at these rolling waves of snow.

The hallway shot straight out behind the main building, with the locker rooms along the back wall and then the gym at the far end. The side facing out was safety glass, floor to ceiling. It looked onto the main road, where it cut off from Route 7, headed down, and leveled out before winding around the front of the building. That made watching easy, at least at first. Most of us hunkered down against the wall, either sitting on our coats or using them as pillows between the wall and the backs of our heads.

As the snow climbed higher against the glass, we had to adjust our positions, sitting up straighter and occasionally craning our necks for a better look. Every once in a while, someone would get up and walk over to the window.

The first thing you saw was that there were no cars going by. It had been that way since I'd arrived, but it was sort of a fresh wound each time. It's not like there were ever many cars out on the little dead-end road that led to the high school and a few houses farther on. It's not like there were ever even all that many up on Route 7, but there were usually, you know, some. Apparently, there'd been a snowplow a little while before Pete, Jason, and I arrived. And there'd been two cars trailing right behind it, riding in its wake, like those little fish that follow sharks.

Not that you'd know a plow had been by, looking out at the uninterrupted field of white that stretched out in front of the school. There should've been a little black ribbon cutting through it, and another one for Route 7 rising up the slope in the distance. But there was no sign of the roads now. There was no way of knowing where they were except memory.

Still, that piece of information told us what to look for. No car was going to be able to bull its way over these roads at this point. One of the big town plows would have to go first. That's what we were watching for: the dull orange of the plow trucks. That's what we were listening for: the sound of metal scraping asphalt, the sound of the plow doing its work.

It's not that it didn't occur to me that this storm might be too much for even the plows now. It crossed my mind. I'd never seen this much snow fall this fast. But I'd never heard of a snowplow getting stuck in snow either. That was like a fish drowning in water: Snow was its element, what it was made for.

The first hour ticked by, and then the second. The cell phones sat next to people like pet rocks. None of us were exactly in a sunny mood, but Gossell was downright angry. He didn't say so, but you could see it in the way his jaw was set. His bearded chin was pushed forward and you could almost hear his teeth grinding. Waiting around with us had cost him his own chance to make it home. I didn't know what kind of car he drove, but it wouldn't matter much at this point.

Walking over from shop, we'd seen a huge lump of drifted snow in the faculty parking lot. It looked like an igloo, and Jason had made some sort of Eskimo joke. The punch line was, "And then you kick the polar bear in the icehole!" It had seemed funny at the time, but now it occurred to me that it must've been Gossell's car under all that snow. And that was hours ago.

And I know Gossell was thinking that it was a lost cause anyway, that we were waiting around for rides that weren't coming until the storm let up. Until the plows could make some headway and the snow wasn't falling faster than it could be cleared. I know he was thinking that because I was starting to think it too. All you had to do was look out the window to catch that drift.

And pretty soon, even that depressing view began to vanish. The light faded early this time of year, even on clear days. I looked at the clock above the drinking fountain. It was around five, but it was already almost dark. It was hard enough to see through the storm during the day, but now it was pretty much impossible.

The light from the hallway projected a few feet out, catching the nearest falling flakes, but beyond that it was just shifting murk. There was too much snow and too little light. We sat along the wall and stared out. Mostly, we were staring at the snow that had climbed halfway up the glass, so we took unofficial shifts, standing and peering out.

We didn't call them shifts or even talk much about what we were doing, but every few minutes someone would get up and look out. From the outside, it would've looked like a gopher poking its head and shoulders aboveground for a quick look. That person would sit down after a while, and a few minutes later, someone else would get up and repeat the process. What else was there to do? You couldn't see much out there, but what we were looking for glowed. For a while, there was nothing. It was Julie who saw them first.

"Hey," she said. She was talking to Krista, but loud enough that we could all hear her. "Are those headlights?"

Everyone got up and looked in the direction she was pointing.

Gossell came over from his own spot, a little farther down the hallway. They were headlights; it was some kind of truck, high enough to chest its way through the snow or carve a path on top of it on fat, chained tires. It was up on Route 7, creeping slowly but unmistakably down the slope, toward the turnoff to the school. The lights were just visible through the falling snow, like two tiny, low-lying stars.

It's hard to explain how exciting this was, or even why it was exciting. It was just one truck out on the road but it sort of seemed like, I don't know, like we were back in touch with the world. Pete tried his phone again, and then Krista tried, and pretty soon, everyone who had one was trying to make a call. Then Pete started talking. Everyone swung around to look.

"Yeah, we're here, by the gym, but I think, it looks like, someone's here to pick us up," he said. It didn't look like that at all, but I guess that was the view he had, staring into his knuckles as he held the phone. And then his line must've gone dead. "There's a . . . Hello? Hey? HELLO?"

"Did you get through," I started. "Were you talking to someone?"

"I think so," he said, and then we just went back and forth.

"Your mom? Your dad?"

"Maybe."

"What? Did you, I mean, did anyone answer?"

"I think so."

"Did you hear, like, a voice?"

"Not really."

"What, then?"

"I just thought I heard someone pick up, like that click thing."

"Like the click when you're disconnected?"

"No," he said, and then, "maybe."

The ones who hadn't already tuned Pete out tuned him out now, making sad little smirks and turning back to the window.

"And why would you say that someone was here to pick—" I started, but he cut me off.

"Wait!" He was looking at the screen again. "Look at this," he said, holding it toward me.

I leaned in, but I didn't understand the layout of the screen.

"What am I supposed to be looking at?"

"The texts," he said, "they're gone."

"Well," I said, "that's something." Now that I'd figured out what I was looking for, I could see that the UNSENT/PENDING folder read "0/0." I pulled back a little. "That's probably a good sign."

"Yeah!" he said.

"Unless they just timed out."

He frowned. They did that sometimes. We turned back to the window, but there was no reason to smile there, either. The headlights had stopped moving. Everyone started speculating out loud about what sort of vehicle they were attached to and why it had stopped. The answer to the second question was pretty obvious, but we were willing to consider any and all alternatives.

Every now and then the lights would blink out, but as quickly as my brain could process the loss, the snowflakes that were lining up to block my view would shift and open, and the lights would be visible again. And then, briefly, there was a flash of red light. A few of us saw it, including Gossell.

"Was that a siren or, what do they call them, a flasher? Like for the police?" said Krista.

"I think those are blue," said Jason.

"Well, a fire truck, then."

"That's no fire truck," I said. It wasn't that big.

"It could be something," said Gossell. "Even a volunteer fireman might have a two-way radio, something we could use."

Use for what? I thought. Who do you call on a two-way radio? The police, the fire department, people like that: emergency people, rescue people. That's when I understood what Gossell was thinking, just how bad he thought this was. It was jarring, like running blind into a moving screen on the basketball court.

"I'm going out there," he said.

It seemed like a bad idea, just way too dangerous. It probably wasn't more than ten degrees out there. You could feel the cold right through the safety glass. That stuff was thick and insulated, but the cold still nipped out at me every time I pressed my face, or even a fingertip, to the glass. So yeah, ten degrees tops, and dark, with snow falling heavily and drifting into small mountains on the ground.

Going out into all that seemed like a lot of risk for a pretty shaky reward. He was taking one for the team, I'll give him that. I felt a little flicker of gratitude, but mostly I just had a bad feeling about it.

He walked back down the hall and picked up his coat. It was a big gray parka, a lot like Holloway's. I wondered if they issued them to all the teachers at the start of winter, like gym equipment, or if both men had just reached the point where they no longer cared what their jackets looked like and had just gone for the warmest thing they could find. I knew they had Big 'n' Tall stores in the city, so maybe they had Cold 'n' Old ones too.

He put his hood up and then zipped the jacket all the way until he was peering out through a little tunnel of fake fur. He stomped into his big boots and buckled them up tight. His dress shoes were probably tucked away in the closet of his room, along with the old maps and broken globes and class projects from, like, 1990.

We followed him like a line of ducklings as he headed down the hall. He grabbed the handle of the double door on the right and rammed his shoulder into its metal frame. It barely budged. He pulled back, creating a little space, and rammed his shoulder in again. It was moving now, and he began kicking the bottom of the frame in between his little bull rushes. He was swearing under his breath the whole time, but he was making progress.

The door opened onto a covered concrete patio, which was the only reason the door could be opened at all. But the snow had blown across the concrete, where kids would stand waiting for the late buses in the nice weather. It had started to drift against the wall where they'd lean and, if they were feeling brave, smoke. So the snow was maybe a foot deep against the door. Beyond that, at the edge of the concrete, there was a four-foot wall of white. It glowed dimly in the light streaming through the glass double doors.

One more kick and the door opened wide enough for him to slide through. Gossell paused and, blink-and-you-missed-it, crossed himself: spectacles, testicles, wallet, and watch. Then he shouldered his way through. The wind slammed the door shut behind him, spraying a little fan of snow across the hallway. Pete, Jason, Julie, Krista, and I stood by the doors as Gossell made his way across the concrete.

We watched as he clambered up the wall of snow. He was kind of nimble for an old guy. Like I said, he was an assistant football coach, so I'm sure he'd been a player back in the day. He reached the top and took a step forward. He took another and sank down up to his waist. I thought he might turn around, but he kept pushing forward into the dark and the snow. He took a few more forced steps, his feet moving unseen under the snow and his upper body leaning forward into it, and then we lost sight of him.

"You really think it was a flasher or something like that?" said Krista as we returned to our spots against the wall. I think she was talking to Pete, but he was heading off toward the men's room at the end of the hall, so I took the opportunity to answer.

"I guess it could be," I said.

"But why would it go off and on like that?"

"I don't know," I said, and that was the end of my latest attempt at conversation with Krista. It was quiet for a few seconds. Some of us took a seat and the others kept standing. My jacket was still warm from the hours I'd already spent sitting on it.

"Can you see him out there?" said Julie.

"I think I can," said Jason, his nose pressed against the cold glass. "Over there, sort of in the middle of the lawn. See how there's movement?"

"Oh, yeah," she said.

"Maybe they just, like, brushed it with their hand," said Jason.

"Brushed what?" said Julie.

"The button," he said, "for the flasher. Like they were reaching for the radio and hit the button for the siren-flasher thing."

"Yeah," I said.

"I could see that," said Julie.

Les let out some air, blowing a dismissive little *tiisss* through his teeth. When he spoke, you could hear the smugness in his voice.

"That's no flasher, no volunteer firefighter," he said. "That red light? It was a flare. For the road, only there is no road right now. That guy up there is as screwed as we are. More."

It was quiet for a few seconds as we turned the idea over in our heads. Then Pete made a *kapow* sound and a hand gesture like he was shooting himself in the head. He knew Les was right. We all did.

"Why didn't you say something before Gossell went out there?" said Julie.

"Why should I?" said Les. "It's his life."

It was, and that was the problem. I don't think it was really Les's fault. I mean, I don't think any of us thought that people would actually die in this storm. We'd been through lots of them, and it'd never happened to anyone we knew. We'd have to change that thinking, though. When we did, we'd all start to think the same thing: that maybe Les had killed a man.

For now, we still had hope. We went back to staring into the darkness.

"Can anyone see him?" asked Krista.

No one could. The headlights burned for a little while longer, and then they didn't. It had been a while since we'd first seen them, and it was tough to say whether they'd faded out over time or had gone out suddenly. It had seemed like they were getting stronger for a while, but that was probably just because it was getting darker around them. They were gone now, in any case. We thought that was as bad as it could get.

And then the power went out.

EIGHT

A half dozen swears crackled down the line where we were sitting, F-bombs going off like fireworks. And then, one by one, cell phone screens popped on and hovered in the darkness like oversized electronic fireflies.

"Check it out," said Pete as he activated his flashlight app. Faces faded in and out of view as he swung his phone in a wide semicircle.

"Ow," said Julie after looking directly at it. "Jerk!"

He swung the beam back toward her and they exchanged small, nervous laughs. When he turned it off, the hallway was dark again.

The lines that brought power to the school from a substation a mile away had come down. They were lying somewhere in the snow, hissing and kicking or just dead and buried. The power lines around here were thick and even ran underground in places. I guess the power company figured that was cheaper than replacing them after every blizzard or ice storm. Of course, not all blizzards were created equal, and I wasn't surprised that this one had brought them down. I was surprised it had taken this long. I think we'd all been waiting for it.

"What just happened?" asked Julie, though it was pretty obvious. She wasn't dumb; she was just talking so she wouldn't feel alone in the dark. Most of the others joined in, but not me, not right away. I needed to think about this, figure out what it meant.

This was real isolation now. They wouldn't even be able to see the school from the road, to see the lights on and realize that people were stuck here. Gossell would know where we were, but a man could get turned around easily in the dark in a storm like this.

And this was absolute darkness: walk-into-walls, trip-over-furniture darkness. I couldn't even see the big white face of the clock above the drinking fountain. The little electric hum it had been giving off this whole time had gone quiet. Its hands had stopped short in their slow crawl toward seven o'clock. As far as it was concerned, time was standing still.

It was winter now, and at this hour it would've been dark anyway. And on a totally overcast day like this, there wouldn't be any last rays leaking over the horizon. I've heard that in the big cities it never really gets totally dark like this, because of all the headlights and streetlights and all of that, but we weren't in a city. We weren't even near one. Our power was out and we couldn't even keep one set of headlights lit and above snow level. We were in the boondocks, the sticks, the butt-end of nowhere.

It seemed like I should still be able to see the snow. I mean it was white, as white as a thing could be. But there was no light for it to catch now, and it was invisible beyond the black sheets of safety glass. It was still falling, though. You could just sort of sense it out there.

You know how sometimes you can tell that it's gray and rainy outside, even if you're not near a window? You know how you can just feel it somehow and it sucks the energy right out of you? That's what this was like, except it wasn't rain and it wasn't draining as much as suffocating. It was like being slowly buried by something quiet and heavy. It was like a cold hand reaching out for your neck in the dark.

All I could see was the double image of the cell phone screens, floating along the wall and then reflected back from the hallway glass, as if our phantom doubles were sitting and facing us three feet away. They flicked on and off, but after a while, they were mostly off.

Then there was nothing left to do but sit there on my coat, thinking dark thoughts. I guess I was sort of wallowing in it, but then I snapped back into the conversation going on around me, because Krista said something that I hadn't thought of.

"What about the heat?"

"Oh, yeah," I said.

"Will it stay on?" she said.

"I think, like, the flame or whatever keeps burning," I said.

"Like on a gas stove. I mean, it's probably lit electronically. It's not like there's some dude down there with a match. But once it's going I think it keeps going."

"But it doesn't keep going, like, constantly, does it?" said Krista.

"Yeah," said Julie. "Doesn't it go on and off?"

I thought about what I knew about furnaces, or maybe it was a boiler? Not much. It seemed like the sort of thing people used to know about. I thought about the furnace at my house, how on cold days you could hear it click on. How it would sort of hum to life and a few seconds later the warm air would start rising up through the vents and you might put your hand there, feel the warmth, and be glad to be inside. And then I thought about how it would click off a little while later, once the thermostat said its work was done.

"Yeah," I said. "I guess."

"Well, will it start up again the next time it shuts off? With the power out, I mean?"

"Is it on now?" someone else said. I wasn't sure who.

"Is anyone near, like, a vent or anything?"

No one was.

"I don't think it will," said Jason. His dad worked on houses for a living.

"You don't think what?" said Krista. "That it will start back up again?"

She was talking to Jason now. Even in the dark, you could sort of hear which way she was facing. I don't think she knew about his dad, but she probably heard the confidence in his voice. It was the sound of someone speaking from experience rather than someone just thinking out loud. And I'm sure that Jason did know more about it than me. He was my friend, but it still sort of stung to be cut out of the conversation like that. I pictured Krista's face, her eyes open wide in the dark, her soft body leaning against the hard wall.

"Yeah," said Jason. "I think it's pretty much done without power. I mean, it's not electric heat, but it needs electricity for other stuff."

I couldn't tell if Jason didn't know what that other stuff was — if he was just thinking out loud like me — or if he did, but didn't want to sit there explaining it to the rest of us. I tried to think what he might be talking about: switches, fans, pumps? I had no idea. It made me think of some big, old factory somewhere, like the kind of place where kids lost their fingers during the Industrial Revolution.

"Well, OK," said Pete. "So it won't relight. Can't we keep it from, like, clicking off in the first place?"

"You mean, like, the thermostat?" said Julie. "Like at home?"

"Yeah," said Pete. "Couldn't we, like, open a window next to it? The heat would keep going then, right? Does anyone know where a thermostat is?"

No one did. At least no one said so. I realized that we hadn't heard anything from Les for a while. I wasn't even sure he was still over there. I hadn't heard Elijah either, but I wasn't too concerned about where he was.

"Wait," said Pete. He said that a lot. "We can use my flashlight app to find one."

It seemed like a good idea to me. Find a thermostat and keep it cold. Of course, it wasn't.

"Won't matter," said Jason.

"Why not?" three of us said at once.

"Hello?" he said. It felt a little unnecessary.

"Yeah?" we said.

"The thermostats are electric."

"What does that mean?" said Julie, and then she got it. "Oh." No power, no heat.

"Well," said Pete. "We are really and truly screwed."

I tried to think of something to add, but I couldn't even do that. I felt angry and helpless and stranded, all at the same time. And then I heard a laugh. It was soft and sort of under-the-breath, but someone was definitely laughing. At first, I thought it was Les and I was going to tell him to shut his face. He can't punch what he can't see, right? But then I realized it was Elijah, and that just creeped me out.

A few seconds later, Les joined in.

NINE

How long could we be stuck here? That was the question now. How long, like, conceivably? We had no power, no lights, and the heat was already leaking out of the building through a thousand cracks and seams and windows.

"It's only for one night," said Julie.

"Tops," said Pete. "The snow could've stopped already."

"We've got jackets," said Krista.

The talk continued along those lines. The tone was: It's not so bad. The tone was: This too shall pass. The tone was: Forced. It was like listening to your mom trying to cheer you up when you knew she didn't really believe what she was saying.

Still, we were going through the motions. If you just started listening now, you might think that we were talking about an overnight camping trip, and a coed one at that. The more we talked, the more we sort of talked ourselves into it. It wasn't so bad.

79

I mean, there was obviously not going to be school tomorrow, so it's not like people would be piling off the buses and tripping over our cold, sleeping bodies. We'd just wait for the storm to taper off, go home, warm up, and spend the day on our couches with blankets and cups of hot chocolate. It'd be a great story: "The Night I Had to Sleep on the Floor of My High School."

"Where do they keep the gym mats?" said Krista, and she said it sort of suggestively, like she was suddenly in the middle of a game of Truth or Dare. I felt my pulse rev a little. I mean, it was dark in here; who knew what might happen?

You know what it's like, right? When your hormones are driving the bus and your brain's sitting somewhere in the back, near the wheel hump? It's not a rational state, which is why I was probably the only one who wasn't completely thrilled when the emergency lights clicked on above us.

It had been maybe half an hour since the power had gone out. I guess the emergency lights were on a delay, so they wouldn't come on every time the power dipped or a fuse was blown. I was sort of surprised the school had them at all. Wasn't this place supposed to be empty at night?

The emergency light above us looked sort of like a big legless crab stuck on the wall. It was basically a tan square, not much bigger than a lunch box. Two bulbs stuck out of the top on little metal stalks. The bulbs were curved like little headlights and pointed out in opposite directions at forty-five-degree angles.

That's what I meant by the crab thing — it looked like a

cockeyed creature looking both ways at once, making sure the coast was clear. My mind kept going that way, constructing a little story: Then it saw seven humans below it and just froze, its back against the wall. I shook it off and refocused before I did something truly lame, like give the thing a pet name.

The light coming out was surprisingly strong. I mean, it's sort of amazing the thing worked at all. It must've been a long time since it'd been on. It's like how people leave flashlights in drawers and forget about them. Then when they finally need them, the batteries are dead. Instead, crisp white light cut through the darkness of the hallway, fading as it went.

"And there was light!" said Jason, and small laughs filled the hallway. Things were funny again. The school was still functioning, and everything was going to be fine. Or maybe that's too much to read into two beams of light, but the mood had definitely changed. It was less forced, more real. We could see each other again. We could see the outlines of our coats and backpacks, like dark puddles on the floor.

There were a few more jokes. Julie told Pete he looked a lot better with the lights out, and they both laughed. Those two sort of knew each other. And then our new optimism led us to the next topic: What else could we do to improve our situation for the night?

"We should go to our lockers," said Krista.

I was vaguely aware that there were emergency lights scattered throughout the school. I tried to remember where I'd seen them, like if there was one near my locker, but they were the sort of things you didn't pay attention to most of the time. I stood up and looked through the glass of the hallway. It was a bad angle, but I pressed my forehead to the cold glass, and I could see some windows along the side of the main building, lit now and just visible through the falling snow.

"I'd like to get my sweatshirt," said Julie.

That kind of brought the topic back to the heat. Was it colder already? It felt like maybe it was. After that, going back to the lockers was an easy sell.

And you might be thinking, Who needs to sell it? If anyone wanted to go back to their lockers, they could just go, right? With Gossell still somewhere out in the storm, there were no teachers to tell us what to do. And all that's true, but for whatever reason it sort of seemed important that we all agreed on these first moves we made. I don't know if it was because of the situation — emergency lights made it an official emergency, right? — or because we were used to being told what to do here or because we were just scared. All I know is that we took our sweet time getting going.

Even once we started making our way toward the lockers, we basically stuck together. I mean, we strung the line out enough so that it wasn't obvious, but no one, not even Les, was ever really out of earshot. It helped that we were all sophomores and freshmen, so our lockers were in the same area. I guess it made sense that we'd be the last ones here. Juniors and seniors wouldn't get stuck waiting for rides. They had their own cars, or friends who did.

Anyway, underclassmen had their lockers in the same few

hallways. The upperclassmen called it Losers' Alley. That stung at first, but you learned pretty quickly that it was better to hang out among your own than to drift into the juniors' and seniors' territory.

"We'll meet back here, OK?" said Krista as the girls headed down the left hallway where the freshmen had their lockers. Of course we would—they were the only girls here. In the half-lit hallway, her voice hit me like a splash of warm water.

We all went to our lockers to forage. The emergency lights were pretty far apart. There was basically one per hallway. On the trip over, things had come in and out of view as we walked. Things would get brighter as we approached the lights in the center of the straightaways, and more and more shadowy as we approached the corners. Pete was up front the whole time, blazing away with his flashlight app. It really was pretty bright, but it seemed puny in the dark patches. It wasn't a real flashlight; it was like a toy. I was still kind of jealous, though.

I was lucky once we reached the lockers: Mine was just a few feet to the side of the emergency light. Not that I really needed it to open the lock. How many times had I spun my combination this year? It was like a reflex by now. Still, the light helped me identify my locker number and rummage through the contents. My locker was a mess. I thought about asking Pete if I could borrow his phone, and then I thought about asking Jason, because he was closer, and just the normal glow from the screen would be enough.

I didn't. To be totally honest, I was a little embarrassed about not having my own phone with me. I thought about it sitting there on my dresser, where I'd left it. I felt like a butt-kissing, capital-L Loser.

In the end, I just pushed my hand around in my dark locker like I was noodling for catfish. I really should clean this thing out, I thought, as I stuck my fingers into a pile of old papers and came back out with a snack-pack of Oreos. When were these from, September? I stuck them deep in my pocket, then looked around to see if anyone had heard the crinkle of the foil wrapper.

Stale or not, this was the only food I had. Really, I had half a mind to scarf the Oreos on the way back, maybe in the shadowy stretches in between lights. But it occurred to me that I might need them for trading. I'm sure some of the others were turning up food too.

I looked over at Les, almost directly across the hall from me, and saw that he had two lockers open. He must've spied on his neighbor and memorized his combination. Or maybe he'd just beaten it out of him. He'd already gone through his own locker and had something folded over his right arm. Now he was pushing through the contents of the other locker, looking for treasure.

I turned back to mine and made another quick pass through it. Nothing. I slammed it shut.

We made our way back to the hallway outside the gym. We were like a band of gypsies, with random scavenged items in our arms: sweatshirts, spare shirts, gym clothes. Anything soft and potentially warm was carried off. Pete had a ski hat with a little pom-pom on top sticking out of the crook of his arm like a limp rabbit.

I remember the morning he'd shown up wearing that thing. We'd ragged him mercilessly about it, and he'd stuck it all the way in the back of his locker. If this storm hadn't happened, he probably never would've taken it out again. Now he was carrying it out in the open, like a prize.

There was no food visible among the prizes, though. Everyone must've made the same decision I had and hidden it. Any sharing or trading would be done later, among friends. I guess this was when we started keeping secrets. Everyone was scanning everyone else's haul, eyes drifting to the side as we passed under a light. Krista had already put her Tattawa Soccer sweatshirt on over her sweater and put her jacket back on over both. It wasn't really cold enough to need that many layers yet. She wasn't bundled up against the cold. She was bundled up against the possibility of cold.

We talked off and on for hours back in the little hallway that had become our base for the night. We talked about a lot of things: Gossell ("He's probably in one of those houses up on the slope, in front of a nice wood fire," we agreed), the buses we would've been on ("Half of them wouldn't make the hills"), the weathermen on TV ("Hilton Kalish, wrong again ... I can't believe they pay that guy").

We watched the emergency light for signs that it was dimming and tested the air for any taste of real cold creeping in. We took short sips from the drinking fountain because there were no emergency lights in the bathrooms. I borrowed Jason's phone for my first trip to the men's room, but the faint blue light wasn't much use. I was a little off target, and I wasn't the only one. By the time I zipped up – with the phone faceup on the top of the urinal, lighting the metal handle – I knew that place was going to be a slippery, stinking mess before too long.

Back in the hallway, we made nests of whatever we had. The lights held for now. I think we all knew that they ran on batteries and that this little reprieve wouldn't last long. But not one of us thought that we'd be here another night. The idea seemed totally crazy.

Every once in a while, someone would check a cell phone. The screen popped on in the dim light, and everyone would look over, but there was never anything to report: no service, no messages, no nothing. We just thought the lines were still jammed or the service was still muffled by all the snow.

Then one of us would walk over to the window and look out at the road. Nothing to report there either, just more snow. You could feel the eyes on you when you got up to look out. At first we said things like, "Still coming down," but after a while, we just said, "Yep." And sometimes a strong gust of wind would rattle the glass, the storm letting us know it was still out there without anyone having to look.

It was pretty clear by then that no one was coming for us that night. Eventually, there was nothing left to do but close our eyes and drift off. It was a bummer, and the sort of fun, sleepover mood from before had been pretty well washed away. We were resigned to a full night of hard floors and dark bathrooms, but we all went to sleep thinking that tomorrow would be the day after. We thought it would be the day the plows cleaned up the big storm, life went back to normal, and we went home. We weren't even close.

TEN

The emergency light was out when I woke up. I was lying so that, when I blinked my eyes open for the first time that morning, I was looking right at it. Was it on a timer, or was it out of batteries already, after just one night? That seemed a little unlikely. Wouldn't the batteries be made to last longer than that? Then again, how old were those batteries?

I looked away from the walls and over toward the windows. It took me a few moments to process what I was seeing. Weak light was streaming in through the top of the glass, running the length of the hallway, maybe eight feet up. At first, my groggy brain thought that must be how the hallway was built, windows at the top, like a basement. Then I remembered that it was a glass hallway, top to bottom. What I was looking at was eight feet of snow, but my brain didn't want to believe it.

The ceiling was probably ten feet high, so what's that, two feet of glass not blotted out by snow? The snow looked black, except near the top, where a little light seeped down to turn it a soft gray. Imagine that: black snow. I knew it wasn't, that it was something about the dim, uneven light in the hallway.

I sat up and looked at it for a while. It was like how you can't see out the window into the darkness at night, but anyone out there can see in, if that makes any sense. Anyway, whatever, it was an optical effect: eight feet of black snow topped by a two-foot band of morning light so dim that my eyes didn't even need to adjust to it. It was bizarre and kind of overwhelming. I felt like I was being buried alive.

I could only see two things in the space above the snow. The first was the dim morning light. I've already told you about that. The second was the snow, still falling.

It didn't look like it was falling as hard as yesterday, so maybe it was tapering off. I was in no mood to get my hopes up, though. I'd gone to sleep sure this would all be over when I woke up, but it had obviously been going gangbusters during the night. I looked at the gap, watched the snow come down, and tried to calculate how long it would be until it was all the way up to the top, until no light would get in. I felt my chest tighten and looked away.

I sat up straighter and got my bearings. It was colder now. I exhaled in a low, steady stream, but I couldn't see my breath, so it wasn't that cold. I'd been sleeping for hours in my jacket, hat, and gloves, so parts of me were actually pretty warm. My hands were sweating; I'd never slept with gloves on before. I took them off now and felt the cool air curl into my wet palms. It felt good and distracted me from the tightness in my back and the bruised feeling in my left hip. I'd been sleeping on my side on the floor and now I shifted my weight to figure out what hurt and what didn't.

I looked around, rubbing the left side of my face to try to get some of the feeling back. The others looked like they were still sleeping. They were curled up or sprawled out on either side of me. The light was still too dim to see colors well, but I could see their shapes. Jason was on his side, drooling into his hand. Pete was wearing his ridiculous hat and had a little smile on his face, dreaming of someplace other than here. Les was farther down, spread-eagled on his back like he was making a snow angel. His chest was rising and falling, rising and falling. We were lucky: no heavy snorers.

I looked over to my left, where the girls were. They were curled up, facing each other like bookends. My eyes swept over Julie and fell on Krista. She was wearing her sweatshirt and jacket but had taken off her hat and placed it under her head so that it was in between the side of her face and the cold tile floor. Her mouth was open just a little, and I could see her nostrils flare in and out as she breathed. She was curled forward with her knees pulled halfway up so that the line of her back and legs formed the shape of an *S*. I looked at the line of her *S* and then I looked at the line of her, well, anyway, that's when I realized Elijah was watching me.

He was watching me watch her. I don't know if I sensed him looking, the way they say you can feel it if someone's staring at you, or if I just did the math and realized I hadn't seen him yet. He was sitting up against the far wall, where the hallway *L*-ed down toward the double doors. He didn't bother to look down when I looked up at him. Why should he? He'd caught me looking, not the other way around.

We sat there looking at each other. It wasn't a staredown, exactly, at least it didn't feel like one. Elijah had this thousand-yard stare thing. He might be looking at you, he might be looking through you. It was tough to tell. Neither of us spoke, and then he raised his right hand to his head and made a plucking motion, as if he was picking something out of his hair. He dropped his hand down to the side and made a motion as if he was letting something go.

I didn't understand at first: There was nothing in his hair and nothing in his hand. Then I raised my right hand to the same spot and, sure enough, the empty Oreos wrapper was stuck to my head. I plucked it off and stuck it in my pocket. The empty foil crinkled as I crushed it down. It wasn't loud but I guess it was enough. I heard movement behind me. Jason sat up and that caused Pete to turn over onto his other side, still chasing that dream.

I nodded to Jason but he didn't see me yet. He was staring at the snow wall. The light coming in through the top was stronger now, and it was brighter in the hallway. The wall wasn't black anymore, it was gray against the glass. I thought back, had it ever really been black?

I turned back toward Elijah, but he was gone. I guess he had wandered down toward the doors. With the snow so deep, I could no longer see around the corner of the glass hallway. But I hadn't heard him go. My head swam for a second. I wasn't sure I trusted my eyes right now. I stood up, just to get the blood flowing, to wake up a little. My knees cracked but it felt good to be up, closer to the light coming in.

"Hey," whispered Jason.

"Hey," I whispered, turning toward him.

He looked out at the snow pressed against the glass, literally tons of it. Then he looked back at me and made the same shoot-me-now gesture as Pete had the night before, but he made it with both hands. Then he dropped his thumbs, shooting himself in both temples.

Good morning to you too.

ELEVEN

The snow was a dull white against the glass by the time Pete woke up. The girls were next and then Les. Elijah drifted back into the fold, and there we were, just like last night, seven kids on our own, hanging out in a little cluster.

"All dressed up and nowhere to go," said Jason.

We were still bundled up in the extra clothes we'd worn to sleep. I walked over to my backpack and put my hat in it. It wasn't that cold yet, maybe fifty-five, and I wanted to have something in reserve. My backpack was against the wall where we'd slept, and now that we were up, we'd all drifted away from that area. I guess we were keeping it separate. It was the "bedroom." Now we were all standing in the "living room" closer to the main doors. I walked back to the group thinking we'd need a new "house" soon.

People were walking up to the glass and standing next to it. They were trying to measure its height based on their own. Best guess: a little over eight feet. I didn't have the heart to tell them it had been a little under eight feet half an hour ago. It wouldn't be long before there was no space for light to come in at all.

Everyone with a phone tried it. When they got nothing, they stood up against the glass and raised their phones above snow level; Krista had to stand on tiptoes. There was absolutely no signal now. In one sense, it was just more of the same, but in another sense it was kind of shocking. It was morning now. It seemed like things should be reset, rebooted. What we didn't know, what we had no way of knowing at the time, was that something had happened overnight. Up on the mountain — at the height of the storm, in every sense — the cell tower had been knocked out.

We just sort of stood around for a while. No one was really sure what to do, apart from swear and kick the wall. At first, the morning got brighter as the sun climbed higher behind the heavy clouds, but then it started getting darker again as the gap at the top of the windows continued to fill with snow. I think we all knew we'd need to move to another part of the school. The light seemed weird and unreal, but everything else seemed strangely clear to me. We were on our own, and we were going to be that way for a while. Gossell hadn't come back. He'd found shelter or, well, he hadn't. The power was out, the phones were dead, the school was losing heat, and it was still snowing. Apart from that, everything was great.

"I've got to take a leak," Jason was saying.

"Well, hurry up," said Pete. "I've got to drop one."

The ground rules had been established last night. One person in the bathroom at a time, in order to avoid pissing on each other's feet or brushing against something you shouldn't.

"There's only so fast I can drain it in the dark," said Jason.

"I'm serious, man," said Pete. "I'm turtling."

I laughed, just because that's such a nasty word. Turtling: when the turd starts poking its head out. And if you're thinking that's not the kind of thing Pete would say around Julie, you're right. The girls were in their own little group. We were clustered together loosely, in groups of ones, twos, and threes. No teachers, no classes, but the cliques remained. We were in little groups drifting inside a larger one. We were like the organs in an amoeba, like the mitochondria, which are the "sites of energy production through ATP." I was fairly sure we wouldn't be having that biology test on Friday.

Krista and Julie were down by the drinking fountain. One of them had a toothbrush and toothpaste and they were taking turns with it. I didn't know a single guy who would bring a toothbrush to school, but chicks were different. I ran my finger along my teeth to see if I still had any Oreo bits in there.

Les was on his own, acting like he didn't care that none of his delinquent buddies were here. All I could say to that was, Thank the Lord. Les on his own was bad news, but he'd been sort of OK so far. There were three of us, all sophomore guys, all friends. We were a natural group and we outnumbered him, but even then, we gave him his space and laughed at the few lame jokes he made.

Elijah was on his own too, but then he always was. He was

hanging out at the far edge of things, like Pluto on those maps of the solar system: just watching, not even really a planet. He was always watching like that, like there was something sort of amusing going on. He was doing it now. Maybe there was something funny about all this, but I didn't see it.

"Oh, man . . ." said Pete.

"Just go to the second floor," I said. There were bathrooms on either end of the second floor in the main building. And since they were on either end of the floor, they had windows. "At least you'll be able to see to wipe."

"Yeah," he said. "Good idea."

He waddled toward the end of the hall, and I walked over to the drinking fountain to see if I could score some toothpaste. "Proper dental hygiene" was honestly the least of my problems, but it seemed like one I could do something about. Just a dab of their Aquafresh on my fingertip and a few seconds at the fountain . . .

Then we'd have to move on to the bigger problem, the one we hadn't talked much about yet. I couldn't ignore it now, though. I felt hollow, almost a little sick. My body was telling me it was time to eat. My stomach had been growling for as long as I'd been up. We'd missed dinner last night and now we were missing breakfast. We'd need food soon. There were seven of us. We'd need a lot of it.

TWELVE

No need to overthink things. If you're looking for food in a high school, there's one place to go.

"It's got to be locked," Julie was saying. "This whole place is locked up tight."

"It'll be, like, double locked," said Pete. "Those big double doors and then the door to the kitchen."

"Dude, we could just hop the counter," said Jason.

"OK, but we still have to get through those honkin' metal doors," said Pete.

"Which ones?"

"You know, where we go in. Where the line is."

"Oh, yeah."

"We could break the glass in the little windows."

Les perked up, looked over.

"I don't think it works like that, like on TV," said Jason. "There's no door handle on those doors, so you can't punch through the glass and open it. It's just got those metal plates to push against."

"Then how do we know it even locks?"

"Dude, have you ever gotten there early? It locks."

"It locks at the bottom," said Krista, joining in.

"What?" asked Jason.

"It's got like a keyhole, one of those round metal disks with a keyhole in the middle, down by the floor."

"Really?"

"Yeah, I was there when they opened up once."

"We could, like, pick it," I said, and was sort of sorry I had.

"Pick it? Alright, 007, go ahead," said Pete, and the others laughed. It was true: I had no idea how to pick a lock.

Julie laughed the loudest, a high-pitched whinny, and that sort of annoyed me. I felt like Pete was just ripping me to impress her. Then again, I'd only started talking to agree with Krista. Being in here with these girls, this could be trouble for us.

"You know what, though," said Jason. It was like when he knew about the heating, he had the same kind of confidence in his voice. He sounded like a car mechanic about to deliver his assessment: blown radiator, broken timing belt. "I bet we could blow out the cylinder."

I sort of knew what he meant.

"With what?" I said.

"Something long and metal," he said. "Like a drill bit and a hammer."

"Uh, anyone got a drill bit and a hammer?" I said, looking around. It was an easy laugh, and I immediately felt like a jerk for getting it at Jason's expense. He didn't care, though. He wasn't as thin-skinned as me, or maybe he just wasn't tripping over himself to impress the girls.

"We could get them," he said, a little smile forming on his face.

"Yeah," said Les. "No problem."

We'd locked the door before leaving shop. We'd turned the little button on the doorknob and swung it closed behind us. But it would be easy to break that window, reach in, and open up. We even had a volunteer. Suddenly, though, I wasn't so sure. I guess I just got cold feet.

"I don't know," I said. "We really want to break in? I mean, we'd be breaking into the shop just so we could break into the cafeteria. That's like one broken window and one blown-out lock, just so we can go scavenge some truly crappy food. Truly crappy food we won't even be able to cook."

That was my big speech, my heroic last stand. It didn't go over well.

"Yeah," said Les. "That sounds about right."

"Dude," said Jason. "We've got to eat."

"Don't be such a wuss," said Les.

I was thinking, Screw you, man, I just don't want to get kicked off the basketball team, but I didn't say it. I held it in and assessed the situation. Jason and Les were all for it, Jason because it was his idea and Les because he wanted to break something. But the girls weren't saying anything. Julie was the swing vote. Krista and Pete would both go along with her, so I sort of turned and started talking in her direction.

"Yeah, we've got to eat," I said. "But we don't have to eat

right now. I mean, what is it, ten o'clock? It's not even lunch and we're going to start busting things up, trying to get at the PB&J?"

"Dude," said Jason. "I haven't eaten since lunch yesterday. Yester-frickin'-day. That's almost twenty-four hours."

"I'm pretty sure the human body can go twenty-four hours without food," I said, sounding uncomfortably like a teacher, that same condescending tone. Why was I being such a jerk to Jason this morning?

"Yeah, but why should we? The food is right there. Right there."

"Let's just wait a while," I said. "At least till it really is lunchtime."

A few people checked the time.

"But what's the point in waiting if we're hungry now?" said Jason.

"What if someone comes in the meantime?" said Julie, and I was glad to have her on my side, but I knew she was going to get shredded for that one.

"Ha!" said Jason.

He walked over and banged on the hallway glass; the snow on the other side towered over his head and didn't even hint at moving.

"Who's coming, snow gophers? Gonna burrow their way in? Gonna dig us out? We're on our own for the foreseeable frickin' future!"

Les was laughing quietly but hard enough that his face was turning red. "Snow gophers," he repeated.

Jason and Les, they were like friends all of a sudden. And I knew it was just because they both wanted the same thing, because I was being lame, but they had a few things in common too, aggression, mostly.

"Let's just wait a few hours," I said.

"Why?" Jason said. He was on a roll now. He had backup, and it was making him more confident.

"Because," I said. I needed something to slow him down, so I tried the truth. "Because I don't want to get kicked off the team, alright? Anything happens in here, it won't be too hard to figure out who did it. We'll all get blamed. I'm not saying we shouldn't do it, I'm just saying we should at least pretend to hold out a little. We go a day without food, who's gonna blame us? We start breaking things down first thing in the morning — it's like we couldn't wait to do it."

Jason didn't say anything for a second.

Sports were pretty big at Tattawa. Most of us played something. Jason actually swung a pretty mean bat. "I just don't want to get kicked off the team is all," I said again, and that clinched it.

"Yeah, OK," he said.

"What time?" said Pete.

"One?" I said.

"Twelve thirty?" said Krista.

"Whatever," said Jason.

"You're all a bunch of losers," said Les.

THIRTEEN

The snow gophers never showed, so a few hours later, we made our way toward the cafeteria. Jason was carrying a hammer and some sort of metal bolt, and Les still had his hat on his hand, like a boxing glove, from when he'd punched it through the window.

Those two had been down to the shop, and Pete had walked through the halls to get to the second-floor bathroom, but the rest of us weren't prepared for how dark the school was away from the glass hallway. It was daytime now, and it seemed like it should be light. But away from the glass hallway the windows were mostly covered, literally buried in snow, and the emergency lights were out now. In most places it was darker now than it had been the night before.

It was a little better in the hallway leading to the cafeteria. Big windows looking out on the courtyard let in some light at the top. It also seemed a little warmer.

"I think we're over the furnace," said Jason.

Pete went over to a vent and put his hand to it. "Yeah," he said. "Something."

We crowded around like it was an exhibit at a zoo: the North American speckled heating vent. A faint current of lukewarm air was lazily drifting out. It wasn't much, but when you put your hand up to it and held it there, you could definitely feel it. I put both hands up and then pressed my palms against my face. It felt good.

"Like the last gasp of a dying animal," said Jason.

And right then I realized why I'd been such a jerk to him: He had leapfrogged me. Definitely. Before yesterday, I'd been a step or two ahead of him. More popular, smarter, better athlete. But now, in this shut-down school, he'd taken the lead. All the things that people sort of held against him were advantages now.

His dad worked some construction and was really maybe a step or two above a handyman, but he'd also taught Jason more about buildings than any of us would ever know. And Jason's fatigue pants and sniper rifle T-shirt and that little whiff of violence hanging around him might have seemed a little ridiculous with late bells and assistant principals around. But now, lights out and on our own, it didn't seem ridiculous at all.

And what was I, a good basketball player? A streaky shooter with decent range? A B+ student, more or less? Now, that seemed ridiculous. So all of this was occurring to me right then, and I guess I was sort of staring at him. He saw me, shrugged his shoulders, and put a look on his face, like, "What? Stop being such a freak."

I let out a little laugh, because I really was being a freak. He smiled and shook his head, and I knew that none of that stuff — about leapfrogging and B+ grades — had exactly occurred to him. And I knew Jason, so I knew that even if it had, he was still my friend.

Les was already kneeling down in front of the big double doors that led into the caf. "Here it is," he said.

He had his finger on a little circle on the bottom corner of the right-hand door. From the way it was catching the dim light, you could see it was unpainted metal. He put his finger on the center and made a little turning motion, showing where the key would go.

"Gimme the stuff," he said, and you could see it caught Jason a little off guard. He made this gesture, pulling the hammer and bolt in closer to his body, like, "Mine."

Les stood up, a good two inches taller than Jason. They didn't look like friends anymore. Jason did some little calculation in his head and handed over the tools. I made eye contact with Jason and he gave me a slight shrug like, "Why not?" I'd been thinking the same thing. Let Les do all the breaking: the shop window, the cafeteria door. Then we can sell him out if we get in trouble for it.

Les was kneeling down and hunched forward on the floor again, and we shifted around so that we could see what he was doing. He put the tip of the metal bolt up against the cylinder of the lock with his left hand, turned his body to allow his right hand some room, and then swung the hammer in a little underhand arc.

BANG!

The tip of the bolt pushed the cylinder maybe a quarter of an inch in.

BANG!

Half an inch.

One more swing: The bolt went all the way in, the cylinder disappeared, and Les slammed his hand between the hammer and the door.

BANG-POP! "OW!"

He stood up, shaking his hand. I truly believe that if anyone had laughed at him right then, he would have driven that bolt straight into their skull. We just stood there as he swore. I looked over at Krista, and she was literally holding her breath.

Once Les had gotten it out of his system, he handed the tools back to Jason. He did it in sort of a here-take-this way that I didn't care for much. Then he turned back around and pushed on the double doors. They swung open easily.

Normally, we went through those doors in a long, slow line, but today we all pushed our way in at once. We were hungry, and the prospect of food was exciting, like Christmas morning and Thanksgiving dinner combined.

And there was something else too, another little thrill. I remember thinking, Well, that's that. We've done it now. We've smashed something, broken in. We might say that Les did it, but it was all of us. He was our device, just like the hammer was his. I remember thinking, We can do anything here now. This place is ours, until someone comes to take it back, someone old and angry.

FOURTEEN

I'll say this about the folks who run the cafeteria: Old blue-haired ladies they may be, but they know how to buy in bulk.

It gave me a weird thrill to hop over the counter. How many days had I spent slowly sliding my tray along that railing, waiting for the globs of pseudo-food and then sliding it all up to the register to pay? Jason, Les, and I hopped over the little flat surface next to that register, between the end of the railing and the wall. We were like the people hopping subway turnstiles in the movies.

Pete reached down and flicked a latch; then he lifted the counter up and back. "Uh, guys?" he said. "It opens." He walked through, followed by the girls and Elijah. Pete was missing the point: I'd flip the thing back down, just so I could hop it again on the way out.

Once we were back in the kitchen area, we started knocking around in the cupboards. The light was a little better back here. The big windows at the back were tall enough that their tops still weren't buried. In fact, everything in here was sort of larger than life. It was like a giant's kitchen. The windows were huge and the cupboards were big metal squares located under countertops that ran almost the entire length of the walls. They had those long metal handles, the ones where you pull on the narrow end and the doors pop open, almost like they're vacuum-sealed.

I was trying to think where I'd seen handles like that before, and then I remembered. Those were the kind of handles they had in the coroner's office on crime shows. You know, for the little compartments where they kept the bodies. In fact, the metal doors under the counter looked like those metal doors. I guess they served the same purpose: keeping things preserved.

"It's people!" I said, popping one open.

The others laughed, and then they laughed louder when I pulled out an enormous can of peaches. It was probably like two gallons of canned peaches and it was really heavy. "The brain!" I said as I thunked it down on the counter.

"What is that?" said Jason.

"'Peaches in Syrup,'" I said, reading the label.

"Oh, man, I love those!" said Jason.

I laughed, but it turned out he wasn't joking. He really liked canned peaches.

It took us forever to find a can opener, and when we did, we felt like morons. It had been right in front of us the whole time. It wasn't like the little openers we had at home; it was this big crank-wheel thing bolted to the corner of the countertop. You put the can under it and then swung the handle around. We'd just figured this out, and Jason was maneuvering the can into position when Julie found the refrigerator. It was a walk-in, as big as a small room.

"Check it out," she said, and we all swung around to look.

She popped the big handle and pulled open the heavy door. It was pitch-dark in there, but we all knew what it was. Les walked in and came back out with a white plastic bucket. He put it down and popped the top: peanut butter.

"Sweet," he said, and we all gathered round and looked at it like we'd never seen the stuff before. He stuck his thumb in, scooped some out, and licked it off.

"Gross!" said Julie.

"Just don't stick it back in there," I said. I said it with a little laugh, because 1) it was an obvious that's-what-she-said line and 2) if Les thought it was an order, he'd cram his whole hand in there. As it was, he just glanced over at me and went back into the dark mouth of the refrigerator. We heard him knocking around back in there, and when he came back out, he had two long plastic sleeves under his arm. It seemed weird to keep sliced bread in the refrigerator, but I guess when you buy it by the ton, it keeps longer that way.

Pete took his turn in the fridge next. It took him forever to find the jelly, even with his "flashlight," but eventually he returned with a huge jar of it. The label was white with big black text that read ARTIFICIAL GRAPE JELLY PRODUCT. It looked like something from the military, totally generic.

"Should we close the door?" said Julie.

"What's the hurry?" said Les.

"You know, so stuff doesn't go bad."

"It's not exactly a heat wave out here," said Pete.

I pushed out some breath but didn't see it. "It's warmer than in there," I said.

"Yeah, OK," said Pete. "But go bad? Just how long do you think we're going to be here?"

"I don't know," I said. "But it's still coming down. Could be another day."

Understatement of the decade.

Pete shrugged, accepting it as a possibility, but said, "Nothing goes bad in a day."

"Uh, milk," I said, lamely. Even as my mouth was moving I wondered how I'd become this lame nanny-man in less than twenty-four hours. I swear I used to be cooler. Earlier, I'd been worried about what would happen when the teachers came back. Now I was worrying about what would happen when they didn't. The only difference I could see between then and now was that the snow still hadn't stopped falling.

"Milk," echoed Jason, letting me off the hook.

I guess I'd always been kind of a worrier, and now I had something real to worry about, something more than whether or not I was going to get a varsity letter.

"Yeah, milk," said Les, turning and going back into the walk-in.

And so that was our first meal in the school: peanut butter and generic jelly sandwiches, with little half pints of milk, regular or chocolate, and syrupy peaches straight from the can. We ate in the hallway by the semiworking heating vent.

FIFTEEN

It didn't make much sense to head back to the glass hallway after our so-called lunch. None of us were in the mood to watch as we got slowly buried, and that made the entire dim-to-dark first floor a severe downer.

"You've got to check out the second floor," said Pete, an expert on the topic since taking a dump up there.

"Do you think the air has cleared?" I joked, but no one else got it.

"It's light," he said, "even in the bathrooms."

"Warm?" asked Julie.

"Hot air rises," said Elijah. It was sort of surprising to hear from him, and it was like, if even Elijah wants to go, we might as well.

And it was the right move, all around. We could see that it was brighter up there before we even got to the top of the stairwell. It seemed to be a little warmer too. Krista had been completely bundled up, but she unzipped her jacket at the top of the stairs. Part of that might have been from climbing the steps, though. We'd spent the last twenty hours or so mostly just sitting around.

I was fine, though: Coach Kielty made us run stairs all the

time, and if it wasn't stairs, it was laps. The joke was that he was a track coach trapped in a basketball coach's body. It was the kind of line that was funny on the first lap and not funny at all by the tenth.

We were in the second-floor hallway now. With her jacket open, the light coming through the classroom doors fell on the front of Krista's sweatshirt, and I could see the curve of her chest underneath. She looked over, and I looked away a little too quick but not quick enough, if that makes any sense.

We could see that it was even brighter in the classrooms, and we were all pretty sick of sitting on the floor in hallways.

"Which one?" said Les, who had reclaimed the tools.

"Gullickson's?" said Krista. "English?"

It was as good as any, a big room right in the center.

"The windows face right out," she said.

What she meant was that they faced out on to the parking lot and the road beyond it, so we would be able to see anyone coming. That was good enough for us. Les did his thing, blowing out the cylinder on the lock with one good whack. He was getting better at that.

We all filed in. It was weird, sort of like class was about to start. People picked out desks, dropped their stuff off to the side, and pulled out chairs. Without even thinking about it, Jason, Pete, and I all went straight for the desks we'd sat in during Mr. Gullickson's English class the year before. We were a little cluster of three smack in the middle of the room.

Krista and Julie sat up front. Les sat in the back. Elijah hovered, considering his options. It was like a conditioned response. We'd been trained: We entered a classroom, and we claimed our seats. Actually, we were double trained, because the other thing people did was check their cell phones. It seemed like they might work: We were higher up now and clear of the drifted snow.

No one got anything, of course, and Pete was having another problem now. "These batteries suck," he said.

Jason looked over at Pete's screen and nodded. "What do you expect? You've been using it as a flashlight the whole time."

"Not the whole time," Pete said, breaking into a quick smile. "I was playing Alien Apokillypse for some of it."

"Moron," said Jason, smiling and shaking his head. He pronounced it with a thick hick accent, like *MOE-RONNNN*. It was just this dumb inside joke between the three of us. We got it from a movie.

Pete checked his battery level one last time, made a weird little smirk, then put his phone away.

Then we all bounced up again and went over to the windows. Pete had told us that morning: "You've got to check out the second floor." He meant I had to check out the view, but I'd ignored him. I figured I knew what snow looked like, but I was wrong.

It wasn't a landscape, it was a snowscape. It just seemed wrong. It looked like the ice planet in *The Empire Strikes Back*, the one where they had that big battle at the beginning. It looked like special effects outside, like a model of the world built to scale and then half covered with spray-on snow. Trees were buried up to the tops of their trunks. Only their branches were visible, looking like snow-covered shrubs off in the distance. A two-story house up on the mountainside looked like a one-story house with an upstairs window for a front door.

That was the closest house, and it wasn't all that close. There was a little string of them up there, running along the road. They were maybe a half mile away, but it might as well have been fifty miles. They were up there and we were down here, with a million tons of snow between us.

Off to my left, a little side building was already almost buried. It was only one story, mostly for vo-ag. There'd be no light in that building: no light, no heat, and no reason to be there.

I faced forward again and let my eyes scan the ground in front of the school. The parking lots, the monument, the so-called "Great Lawn," it was all just flat, featureless snow. Anything could be under there, anything or nothing. And out in front of that, the road was a long, barely visible depression in the snow, like a huge wormhole had collapsed under the surface. You could almost see it filling in as you watched it. Soon, even that would be gone, and there would be no way to tell that there had ever been a road there.

That thought bothered me, the idea that you wouldn't be able to tell where the road was. I don't know why, I guess it was just the most obvious sign that we were cut off, isolated, and maybe forgotten.

"Look at that," said Pete. "You see it?"

"What?"

"The smoke."

128

And sure enough, there was a plume of dark gray smoke snaking up from the chimney of the nearest house, the one with the window for a front door.

"Oh, yeah," I said. "Lucky bums."

There were no lights on, but at least they had a reliable source of heat.

"Think Gossell's in there, throwing another log on the fire?" said Pete.

I pictured him in there, his big coat drying over the back of a chair. "Yeah," I said. "Old dog."

The snow was still falling steadily. As I tried to look through the shifting flakes to see if I could see maybe some candles or something in the windows up there, I realized there was something else in the air. Little sounds came through the window now, a thousand tiny clicks and ticks. It was too small to be hail. It was freezing rain mixed in with the snow.

We sat back down, but I could still hear the tiny drops of ice bouncing off the glass when no one was talking. Freezing rain meant it was warmer, but it was sort of a good news/bad news situation. It would leave a nasty crust of ice and heavy snow eight feet up. Like the crunchy topping on my mom's mac and cheese, I thought.

As soon as the thought entered my mind, I shook it out again. I needed to stop thinking about things like that. Home kept creeping into my head now. I was thinking about my house and worried about my mom, but there was nothing I could do about it. There was nothing I could do about it, and no way to get there, so I tried to put it out of my mind.

"The bathrooms are heaven," said Julie, returning to her seat. "A little cold on the ol' butt-cheeks, though!"

I laughed along with the others. It felt good to laugh again.

"Where's Elijah?" she said, looking around.

"Who cares?" said Pete.

"He's with Les," said Krista. "They're opening another room."

"Detention?" said Julie. Everyone laughed. Everyone except for Jason, and when I saw he wasn't, I stopped.

Elijah had considered his seating options in here and chosen none of the above. I didn't know if Les had come to the same conclusion or if he just wanted to break another door. Either way, this was when we started splitting up.

SIXTEEN

At first, it felt good to sit around and talk, in real chairs, in a room brighter and a little warmer than where we'd just been. But after a while, we all got kind of restless. We were like fish in a bowl. Sitting in here, looking out the window, only made that clearer. So one by one, we got up and found things to do.

"I'm completely bored," Jason said to Pete and me at around two thirty or three. "I'm gonna go down and work on the kart."

"Think there'll be enough light?" I said.

"Should be," said Jason. "It's got those big windows, like in the caf."

"Yeah," said Pete, "and it's right up against the back of the school. It's got that, like, slope."

He put his fingers together and speared them down at a forty-five-degree angle toward the floor. He meant that the snow would run down the slope that headed toward the playing fields.

"Maybe," I said. "Could drift."

"Well, I guess I'll find out. Not asking you two to go anyway."

"Good," said Pete. "'Cause we're not."

I was a little annoyed at Pete for speaking for me like that, especially since he wasn't really thinking about me when he did.

133

He was looking over at Julie, like he'd been doing in quick little glances since we all sat down.

It was kind of weird. Jason, Pete, and I were good friends, but a day in, it seemed like we were already getting on each other's nerves a little. Maybe it was because we were all so crammed together. Maybe it was because there were girls here and that made us instant competitors. Or maybe it was because we were starting to realize that we might be in big trouble. Not the school kind of trouble, the real kind. Anyway, Jason got up and left.

"I'm gonna..." said Pete, nodding toward the girls at the front of the room.

"Go on over," I said.

"Dude, come with me," he said. He was sort of whispering now. That was dumb because it was guaranteed to draw the girls' attention.

"Nah, I don't think so," I said, lowering my voice to match his, but trying to sound like I didn't care one way or the other.

Pete turned his head toward the girls again. Maybe I should go over there with him, I thought. I might get a chance to talk to Krista. In fact, that was pretty much guaranteed, given that we were the only four left in here. But what would I say? Without even thinking about it, I reached up and touched the big, honking zit that was bubbling up under my right cheek. I'd felt the beginnings of it when I'd woken up that morning, but now it was bigger and hurt a little to touch.

I pulled my hand down just before Pete turned back.

"You go ahead," I said. "Gonna hit the can."

"Come on, Weems: wingman!"

"What do you want, man? Nature calls."

I went to the bathroom and put a dot of Oxy on my zit. I was going to spread maybe a little more on the other cheek. For some reason, I tend to get really symmetrical zits. I have no idea why, but if I get one on the right side, I usually get one on the left side too, right around the same spot. I'm, like, a medical oddity. Maybe they should cut me up and study me. I heard the little flakes, icy again, scratching off the frosted glass of the bathroom window. Maybe they'd get the chance.

I looked down at the little rolled-up tube of Oxy. I pinched into the plastic in a few places. There wasn't much left. I needed to save it for actual zits. The one on my cheek was going to be a monster, and there'd be others. My skin can barely go a day without betraying me.

When I went back, Pete was still sitting by himself in the middle of the room. I figured if I walked over there, we'd just pick up right where we left off, but it didn't seem like I had a lot of options. I walked over and sat down, but Pete had something else he wanted to talk about.

I guess it was on everyone's mind. "Jason's dad, huh?" he said, leaning in. He was still whispering, but for a different reason, because the same conversation could apply to Krista's mom. That was just one of the reasons we weren't talking much about our parents. The other big one: We didn't really know anything and had no way of finding out.

Obviously, I wouldn't want anything bad to happen to anyone's parents, but it's natural to worry about your own family first. I couldn't have talked to Jason or Krista about this, but I

135

was just glad that my mom hadn't been on the road when it really started to come down. At least she wasn't on the road as far as I knew. Which wasn't far at all. We just didn't know, and all talking about it would do was maybe piss off the others and make me sound like a mama's boy.

But Pete'd brought it up, Jason wasn't around, and Krista couldn't hear. For ten minutes, we talked about our houses. We talked about how high they were, both two stories with a little bit more for the attic. We talked about food supplies and fireplaces. With teenagers to feed, both fridges were stocked full, but my mom was a little better off because there was just one of her.

"But they're in town," Pete was saying. "Things will be better in town."

I'm sure he was right, but they'd still be snowed in without power. I didn't really want to think about my mom sitting in the dark and living on Doritos, much less talk about it. I caught a break there. The emergency lights blinked back on in the hallway. I guess they were on a timer or some kind of off-again, on-again delay.

I got up to go look, and so did Krista. It was like one from each group. We got to the door at the same time and ducked our heads out into the hall to look. As we pushed through the door, our jackets brushed against each other, nylon on nylon, and my hand brushed her thigh. It was an accident or, I don't know, maybe it wasn't. In any case, it happened fast and she didn't say anything. Across the hall, one room down, Elijah prairie-dogged his head out for a look and then ducked back in.

136

He'd sized it up like we all had. It was a huge waste, especially since you could tell just by looking that the power was running down. The light was duller now, less the bright yellow-white of last night and more a dull gold. With no power to recharge them, those old batteries wouldn't last much longer.

As far as I knew, neither Les nor the girls had been planning to go downstairs, but they all headed down there now. It was just kind of an instinct, I guess, not to waste the electricity. And Julie's mind must've kept going down that road, because just before we all split up, she said, "A radio."

And she was right, there had to be a radio in here somewhere, just a little battery-powered thing. I thought I remembered hearing one in the office. It would have news and weather, but I guess the weather was the news at this point.

"I'll go with you," said Pete, and I swear Julie smiled, just a little, and just for a second, but still. Lucky dog.

"I'll go to the caf," I said, "bring back some more food."

The others looked at me, sizing up the plan.

"We won't want to go once it gets dark," I added.

"Well, I guess I'll help foodman here carry the stuff back, then," said Krista. I'd sort of assumed she was going to go with Julie and Pete, but maybe she didn't want to be a third wheel. Now she was going with me. Just like that, I went from being jealous of Pete to being kind of grateful.

"I guess we need the locksmith," Pete said to Julie, and they made these matching "Uh-oh" expressions before heading over to Elijah's room to get Les.

"Did I miss something?" Krista sort of whispered to me.

"Seriously," I said, because I was thinking the same thing. It was like Pete and Julie were a couple already.

"Well, won't that be cozy," she said as we headed back down the stairs. "Just the three of them."

I laughed, and I probably laughed harder than I should've because, you know, hot chick. But there was something else. The day before, I'd been half afraid just to be around Les. He'd seemed barely under control when the school was full and everything was in working order. And now, empty, with no rules and no one else his size? But a day in, we'd started to see him as just the kid who opened doors. It worked for us, and he seemed to like it.

Anyway, I had something else on my mind at the moment. I was alone with Krista for the first time, even if we were just fetching food.

"So, it's Weems?" she said.

"Scotty is fine," I said.

"Yeah," she said. "Good choice."

We made a right at the bottom of the stairwell and headed toward the cafeteria. It was colder and darker down here now. It was like night had come early. The emergency lights were wasting their juice on the second floor, but they were the only reason we could see at all down on the first.

I'd made sure I was walking on Krista's right, but I could see now that it wouldn't matter much. Weak light is a zit's best friend.

The snow reached the top of the windows now. It felt like being buried. The windows looked out on to nothing, as if some idiot had installed waist-level windows in a basement. The light from the emergency lights faded in and out as we moved past one and toward another. It was gold now, piss-colored.

"Are these lights, you know?" said Krista.

"Yeah, it looks like it," I said, and it did. It looked like the lights down here were weaker.

"Maybe they came back on sooner down here?" she said.

"Yeah, could be. Could be a different circuit or whatever. Or they could be older down here. The batteries could be further along. Or maybe it just seems that way because it's, like, darker down here."

"We should ask Jason," she said. "When we see him."

I guess it was pretty clear that I had no idea what I was talking about, that I was just thinking out loud again, but it still kind of stung.

"Lights'll be out by then," I said, and she moved a little closer to me as we walked. It was probably just instinct. No one wanted to be alone in the dark. It wasn't much, just half a step in, but we touched as we turned the corner.

It was weird being down here with her. Nice, but weird. A day ago, I'd settled for staring at the back of her neck on the bus ride to school, but then, a day ago, there'd been no shortage of boys stealing looks at her. Now there was a shortage of boys, just in general. There was a shortage of boys, of girls—and of heat and light, for that matter. Her choices were down to going to the cafeteria to help me lug PB&J, hanging with spooky Elijah, or sitting in an empty room and watching it dump snow on our heads for a second straight day.

I had this long talk with Jason about this once, and he said that chicks our age don't think the same way: all about limited options and what you can get. We'd argued about it, because I think maybe they do. I think they're just not as desperate about it. Anyway, what did the two of us know? I wasn't dating anyone, and Jason was dating his go-kart.

So it wasn't a date, and I knew that. And I knew she didn't have many other options. Still, I was walking alone through a half-lit hallway with her. I knew she was cold, and for a second, I had a thought. Just after we bumped together rounding that corner, I thought about putting my arm around her. I'm not nearly smooth enough for that, and it probably would've been a disaster, so I didn't. But just the thought of it — the thought and the opportunity, I guess — was enough to get me going.

The big double doors were still open when we got to the cafeteria, but the heating vent just outside there had died completely. This time I didn't jump the counter: I felt around for the latch and lifted the counter up for Krista.

"After you," I said.

Yeah, it was pathetic, but there was no one around to call me on it.

It wasn't as bright in the kitchen now. The snow was farther up the windows and the sun was lower. We started with the coroner's doors under the counters, but most of that stuff was canned. We wasted a good fifteen minutes looking for a can opener that wasn't huge and attached to the countertop. When we found one, it was about the size of a worn-down pencil. I guess everything had to be extreme in here: too big or too small.

We decided to go light on the canned stuff, because it was heavy and because it would take forever to open the ginormous cans with our little mini-opener. I also wasn't too sure about that "syrup" everything was packed in. It was probably made from like horse bones and toxic waste.

Then we went into the walk-in fridge before the light got too dim. We took turns going in, handing her cell phone back and forth to use the glow from the screen as a light. It probably would've made more sense to have one person get more familiar with it, but we took turns because it was like we were playing a game. It was sort of like Hide 'n' Seek, except this one would've been called Find d' Jelly. We didn't take anything that needed to be cooked, but we did find some cold cuts that seemed safe. There was no mayo that we could find, but that was probably just as well.

Pretty soon we had all we could carry. Apparently, Krista wasn't content just to be better looking than me. She had to be smarter too. She'd emptied out her backpack and brought it along. That hadn't occurred to me, so I just had to grab as much stuff as I could and sort of cradle it all against my chest.

Anyway, it was fun. At one point, Krista was carrying the two jumbo-sized cans we'd picked as keepers: one of peaches and the other of chocolate pudding. That's what you get when you let a freshman and a sophomore do your food shopping. So, she's leaning back and carrying them toward the counter and I go, "Man, you've got some big cans!"

And she was like, "And you've got some mysterious meat," because I was holding something called Potted Meat Food Product.

We laughed, caught our breath, and then started laughing again. We left the meat product behind though. That stuff hadn't even been refrigerated. Weird.

A few times, when it seemed to be going really well, I thought I should try something. My mind was like: make a move, make a move, make a move! Would I ever get a better opportunity?

"Krista?" I said.

"Yeah?"

We were just a few feet from each other. . . .

"Regular or crunchy?" I said. I couldn't quite pull the trigger.

SEVENTEEN

"So, Scotty, you ever heard of a storm like this before?" Krista was asking.

"No, never. I mean, I know there are places in like Buffalo and Alaska where they get like sixty feet of snow a year. But that's a full year."

"Yeah, I know, but that's nothing like this storm. This is like ten feet in a day."

I was trying to figure out how many inches per hour that was, but between that and balancing all the stuff in my hands and talking, the numbers just flew out of my ears. "You ever been up there, to like Buffalo or wherever? It's because of the lakes they get so much snow."

I was vaguely aware that I was speaking like a third grader.

"I used to live there. Well, near there."

"Seriously?" I said. Take that, third grade.

"Yeah, Watertown."

"That's pretty far north, right?"

"Yeah, and right near the lake. They should call it Snowtown. It's like basically Canada."

"You see any moose?" I said, and she laughed. I was amazed because no one seemed to get my dumb jokes.

"They're called meese," she said. "One moose, two meese."

I let out a little snort of laughter. That was something I'd say too. And I was feeling pretty good right then. Like I'd forgotten about my zit, and I was feeling a lot more comfortable around her and not nearly as nervous. The only problem I really had was the ache in my shoulders from lugging the food.

And then we heard voices as we approached the bend in the hall, and it all came back. I remembered we were stuck in our high school and divided into these groups, and there were certain things you couldn't say to certain people, and just the whole general tidal wave of crap. So much for the meese.

The light was murky when we turned the corner, but I already knew who it was. There was a weird echo in the hallway, but I could still make out the voice. It was Les, and my chest tightened a little. I was sort of getting more comfortable with him, but not down here in the dark. He was talking to Julie, and Pete was a few feet away. They were outside the nurse's office.

I was just in the nurse's office two weeks before. I didn't remember there being a radio in there, but it turns out they already had the radio. It came into view a few steps later, dangling from Pete's left hand. I guess they'd taken the one from the main office. I remembered it now. The secretary was always listening to it in the afternoons.

I was wondering what they were looking for in the nurse's office. Then it hit me: blankets. So they were good scavengers, but things weren't going well between the three of them.

"Hey, girl, wanna hold my tool?" said Les, holding out his door-opening gear. It was one of those comments that could be funny or not, depending on who said it and how the girl took it. Or how her would-be boyfriend took it.

"Shut up, man," Pete said, taking a step toward Les. Or, let me rephrase that: Taking a step toward the much larger guy who still had a hammer and a steel bolt in his hands and Lord knows what else in his pockets.

Uh-oh, I thought. Or maybe I actually said it, because just then all three of them looked over toward Krista and me. I guess it could've been the sound of our sneakers that gave us away.

Les looked over, sized us up, and then turned back toward Pete. He sort of cocked his head and looked at him, like dogs do when you make a noise they don't understand. I guess it was disbelief, like: Did I hear that right? Did you just tell me to shut up?

Pete was standing his ground, but just barely. His feet were planted, but every other part of him was leaning back. He had this weird little look on his face, somewhere between the fear of what was about to happen and the acceptance that there was nothing much he could do about it.

"Hey, guys," said Krista, acting like she didn't see what was going on. "Whatcha doin'?"

I was waiting for Les to make a fist and use it, but he was pausing now to process the words. I was already picturing the effects of the punch and just hoping he kept the hammer out of it. Either way, I'd have to do something once it landed. I was having trouble thinking of anything that didn't involve me dropping all this food, running in there, and getting my clock cleaned too. Maybe I could get in one good shot with the peach can?

I was trying to come to terms with this kamikaze mission.

Pete was my friend: I had to do it. But sometimes it's like, Thank God there are girls around, you know? This was one of those times. Krista just kept at it. "Hey," she said. "Hey!"

Finally, Les looked back in her direction.

"Hey, Les," she said. "Hey, Jules."

She didn't mention Pete, and I guess that snub was like a victory for Les or something? I don't know. I don't know where girls learn this stuff. I do know you can't underestimate the power of a pretty girl's voice on a teenage boy, no matter how tough he is. Krista was just a freshman, but she'd pretty clearly figured that out already.

Les sort of half turned toward her.

"What's up?" she said.

He turned the rest of the way.

"How's the treasure hunt going?" she continued.

"We found a radio."

At first I assumed it must've been Pete who'd said that, but he was still standing there with that same expression on his face. It was Les.

"Show her, doughboy," he said. Sometimes people called Pete that because his last name was Dubois. Realizing he wasn't about to get crushed, Pete unfroze and raised the radio up into the uneven light.

"It's got batteries, but the reception's crap," Les added.

"Maybe it'll be better upstairs," said Krista. "Where it's less . . ."

"Buried," I said. It seemed like about time to join the conversation.

"So whatcha doin' here?" said Krista.

"Blankets?" I said. She looked over at me, like: Are you going to be completing my sentences from now on, or can I do that myself? But it didn't seem like a bad thing.

"Yeah," said Les. "You're not as dumb as you look."

And that was another sentence that could be taken either way, but I took a chance and said, "I don't know. I can look pretty dumb...."

And he laughed, and there was just no meanness in it at all, and all of a sudden I was like, Holy crap. Because I'd just realized something about Les, about the kind of trouble he got into and why. Now I understood how he could share a room with Elijah and not rip that scrawny little dude into scraps.

I looked over at Krista because she'd already realized this, and I was just like, How? How on earth would you know that? When did you even deal with this guy before? And she looked back at me, and her look just said: Boys are ridiculous.

For the record, I've never denied that.

"Well, let's get to it," she said. "Those lights aren't getting any brighter."

And they weren't. I wondered how much longer they'd last. Another day, maybe? I guess it depended on when they shut off again. I heard a pop and looked over. Les had knocked the cylinder out of the door lock with one shot.

I walked over to Pete and fake punched him in the gut. It was one of our ways of saying hello. I was just saying, I'm here, man. He gave me a weak little smile.

Les pushed the door open and we all filed in. The nurse's office was a gold mine.

EIGHTEEN

We'd all pulled chairs into a semicircle around the radio, which was set up on a desk in Gullickson's room. Even Elijah had joined us for the occasion. Jason was working the dial.

He'd spent the afternoon working on his go-kart until it got too dark in the shop, I guess. We'd actually sort of waited for him. We didn't have a lot of events around here, and it seemed a little cruel to leave him out of this one. Plus, a quick look out the window told us there was no hurry.

The road out front was still buried, with another foot or two on top of what was there before. There was still no movement up on Route 7, and the house on the hill that was closest to us was up to its gutters in snow. I couldn't see any smoke coming from its chimney like I had before. Maybe it was just too dark, but I didn't think so.

More to the point, it was still snowing. Was it harder or softer than before? I just had no idea. It was all starting to look the same to me, and I was already sick of trying to gauge it. It would lighten up for a few minutes and you'd think maybe this was it, you know? And then two minutes after that it was coming down twice as hard. It was almost better not to look.

The radio was black and boxy, with a telescoping antenna that we'd pulled out all the way. At first, it offered us a wide variety of static, but part of that was because Jason was working the dial too fast. At least I think he was. It's not like I had much experience with old radios with dials. I mostly just listened to the radio in my mom's car, and that one had buttons and "auto-seek" and all that. This one seriously looked like it was from the '80s or something. Finally, Pete was like, "Slow down there, Flash."

Once he did, we started to get little slivers of actual human voices. The first thing we landed on was technically a recorded voice, I guess, but it was still something:

"This is an official announcement of the Emergency Broadcasting Network. A severe nor'easter has stalled over southern New England. Conditions are extremely hazardous, with deep snow and high winds. Stay off the roads. Conserve heat and food. Under no condition should you attempt to leave a functioning shelter. Authorities are aware of the situation and will assist those judged to be in the most danger first. Repeat: This is an official announcement of the Emergency Broadcasting . . ."

The voice repeated the whole thing again, and then there was a long electronic beep or tone or whatever. It was really loud and piercing. I guess it was designed to get people's attention, but it wasn't great when everyone was already leaning in to hear every word. We leaned back and started talking, pretty much all at the same time.

A nor'easter . . . You couldn't grow up around here and not know more or less what those were, but now people started trying to mesh their "more" with the other guy's "less," and Les actually seemed to know more than most of us.

"It's like a machine," he was saying, "like a wheel. And part of it is coming up over the water and part of it is coming down, and so it's like rotating and gaining power and sort of, like, swirling."

"That's a tornado," said Julie, but she was wrong.

"No, these are slower and a lot bigger," he said. "Like a thousand times bigger. They just keep going 'cause there's all these different, like, air currents and clouds, and it all just blenders up and . . . turns to snow."

"Why?" said Julie. "Why would it just turn to snow?"

"'Cause it's cold?" Les said. He had reached the end of his knowledge on the subject.

"It's 'cause there's cold air coming down from the north," I said. I'd seen something about this on TV the winter before. "It's formed between two big, like, masses of air—or, wait: air masses. Anyway, one's warmer and one's colder. That's why it rotates like that. It's, like, opposing pressures. The warm air picks up moisture out over the ocean, but when it rotates into the colder air coming down, that moisture freezes and gets too heavy, so it dumps it. But there's still that pressure pushing it along and more warm air coming in behind it, so it rotates back down. Then more of the warm, moist stuff rotates up and around, and the whole thing starts over again. It just does it over and over until it breaks up or moves on or runs out of energy."

I paused for a second, mainly to catch my breath, but also because I wasn't entirely sure of all of it. Last winter was a long time ago, and it had just been some little segment on the news. I was kind of hoping someone would correct me, but no one did.

"That's what I just said," said Les.

"But where does it get the energy?" said Julie.

I waited for someone else to answer, but no one did, so I went on: "From the fronts? From the difference between the warm and the cold?"

But by then, I really had reached the end of what I knew, just like Les had. The beep came back on, and we turned our attention back to the radio.

"Try another station," said Krista.

"Try WKAR," said Pete.

WKAR was the only local radio station the three towns that fed into Tattawa had to offer. It was located in an old train station in downtown Little River. In fact, Little River being what it was, the radio station was about one-fifth of the downtown district. The station, the post office, the town hall, and a few little stores, one of which was a tiny antiques shop that was only open on weekends. Still, there was the radio station: "99.9 on your FM dial!" It broadcast the high school football and basketball games and ran these really embarrassingly amateur ads for local businesses. It would be like one of your classmates' dads advertising the pizza place in a fake Italian accent.

"They're not going to be broadcasting," I said, and they weren't.

Jason moved the dial slowly now. We all watched the little line crawl over the backlit numbers. It could not have been more perfectly centered: halfway between 99.8 and 100. And still, all we heard was static.

"Transmitter's probably down," said Jason.

"Yeah," said Les. "That little place is buried."

Everyone except Elijah offered an opinion about what to try next.

During our trip up the dial, there'd been no wacky drive-time DJ's, no crappy oldies. I don't know if the stations weren't broadcasting or if the storm was just smothering our reception. I'm sure it didn't help that the radio was a piece of junk. But when we got to the big classic rock station out of Hartford, we got something. It was faint, but it was an actual, live human being. Jason held up his hand and Pete and I gave him five.

Jason turned the volume up and we leaned in. Even before we could make out what the guy was saying, it was pretty clear that the man was rambling. Part of his voice fading in and out was the radio, and part of it was him. He sounded distracted, like he was talking to himself, and I think maybe he thought he was. He probably didn't know if his station was broadcasting either, but it was, and seven kids were hanging on every little stutter and hesitation.

"Man oh man oh man oh man," he was saying. "It is nasty out there, seriously nasty."

He sounded tired and his voice was a little hoarse, and I wondered how long he'd been talking. Had he been stranded there for the whole storm like we were? But he was in Hartford. It couldn't possibly be as bad there. I mean, in a city, the buildings are connected and stuff like that. There are walkways and overpasses, so people could still get around. Still, it was pretty clear that the next shift hadn't arrived for this guy.

"I'm looking out the window now," he continued. "Not much happening in The Insurance Capital of the World. And I hope

157

everyone's homeowner insurance is in order. Home . . . auto . . ."
He stopped short of saying "life."

"I see one guy out there, skiing down the middle of the frickin'
road. And, yep, he just fell over. It's funny, he really does look
like an ant from up here. And he's up! He's up, ladies and gentlemen. Covered in snow. He looks like a powdered donut. I hope
that dumb son of a gun has someplace important to be, because
he should not be out in this. And he's down again."

A gust of wind rattled the windows, like it'd been doing ever
since we'd been in this room, and I could picture that lone skier
out there.

"And he's up . . . he's down. I can't watch this. Again, folks, I
can't emphasize this enough. Stay inside if at all possible. The
snow is up to, well, last I heard it was eleven feet in downtown
Hartford and higher in outlying areas."

I looked around at the others because it didn't get much more
"outlying" than this Podunk school on a dead-end road out in
the middle of what used to be farmland. I could barely see their
faces, though, and I realized that the emergency lights out in the
hallway had blinked out again. I thought about saying something but everyone was just watching the weak glow of the
radio dial.

"And that's on top of what was already there. If you're in a
single-story or ranch-style house, you need to be thinking about
ventilation. Keep your chimney clear, if you have one. This is
dense snow, and there are some layers of frozen stuff in there.
Air won't necessarily make it through on its own."

Les slammed his fist down on a desk and swore. Elijah looked up at the ceiling and mumbled something. They lived in single-story houses, I was guessing.

"Heck, stick a broom up through there. The important thing is just to wait it out. This storm is, and I'm quoting the National Weather Service here: 'unprecedented.' I guess there've been some historical cases but . . . Anyway, these things require lots of energy" – what I'd been saying before, except this guy seemed to know what he was talking about – "and that energy can't last forever."

And then the guy sang a few words of a song: *"Forever! Forevvvv-errr!"* And I recognized his voice, even if it was tired and hoarse.

"It's Andy," I said.

"Holy crap," said Pete. "You're right."

Yeah, it was Andy, one half of Randy & Andy, the station's star personalities.

"I wonder where Ran –" Pete began, but the girls shushed him, and Les gave him a look with the same message.

So we turned back to the radio and listened for a while more, until Andy's voice cracked one time too many, and he put on "Born to Be Wild." We sat there and listened to it, which was kind of dumb and useless, but really, who doesn't like that song?

His voice came back on afterwards. I guess he'd had a glass of water or something. "And that was Steppenwolf, of course. But seriously, folks, do not get your motor running. Do not head out on the highway. Stay where you are. That is the advice we're getting from the State Police. They are beyond swamped and won't be able to assist you in most cases. They are waiting for this to pass, just like we all are."

And so we basically knew we were on our own for the duration. Seven kids in an enormous high school, with blankets and enough food to feed four hundred people for a week? And meanwhile, people were in danger of suffocating in their houses, so why would they rescue us? Where would they rescue us to?

"The National Guard has been called in, but no sign of them yet, not even downtown. I wouldn't be waiting for Uncle Sam, folks. You know those weekend warriors have two left boots. . . ."

"Screw you, Andy!" said Jason. He was not going to listen to a radio personality bad-mouth men in uniform. Any men, in any uniform. "Let's try another station."

But we didn't. Andy may have been one half of a goofball comedy team five days a week, but he had become an actual newsman, on his own and under backup power. And he was getting information from somewhere, official information.

We were hungry, though, and we needed to make dinner while there was still enough light coming in through the windows. We didn't know when or if the emergency lights would come back on. Maybe because of that, it occurred to us to turn the radio off while we ate. The radio was old, and there was a decent chance the batteries were too.

We sat there in silence and near darkness, eating sandwiches. We had a choice this time, cold cuts or PB&J. Most of us went with the flat, slimy cuts of meat, because it seemed like, even as cold as it was getting in here, we should eat that sooner rather

160

than later. Then we ate pudding straight out of the can. We'd found a jumbo-sized roll of plastic wrap along with the food, and after we finished, we wrapped the leftovers up tight and put them on a windowsill with the rest of the food.

Up against the window was almost as good as in a refrigerator. I put my palm against the windowpane: It was bitterly cold outside now, and you could feel the bite right through the glass. A gust of wind bounced the window against my hand and seemed to rock the whole building.

We listened to the radio for a while after that. Some guy was filling in for Andy now, taking short shifts. It was just some other guy from the building, not even from the station. The guy was nervous and hard to listen to. I guess Andy knew it too, because he was playing more music. He didn't seem too concerned with the playlist either. It was supposed to be a classic rock station, but that'd kind of gone out the window. There was some new stuff and some Top 40 and even some country mixed in — like that rock sort of country — and all of it was better than listening to the wind tear into the side of the building.

But mostly it was classic rock. When they played "Atlantic City" by Bruce Springsteen, Pete talked our ears off about "The Boss." Pete had been born in New Jersey and was, like, weirdly proud of that fact.

"The Boss was born in New Jersey, you know," he said.

"Yeah, so was Snooki," I said.

I meant that as a put-down but I'm not sure he took it that way. I wasn't even sure it was true. I can't keep track of all those reality TV stars, except for athletes, which is kind of the same thing. I mean, it's real and it's on TV. Those guys have talent, though, not just egos and nose jobs. I ran through the Celtics' schedule in my head: They were playing tonight. And they were on a West Coast swing, at the Lakers, so they'd definitely get the game in. It didn't seem strange to me that people were playing basketball with this huge storm going on. It seemed strange to me that I wasn't.

Anyway, a Lady Gaga song came on after that. It was catchy and the girls were into it, singing along with the chorus, but if Lady Gaga is classic rock, we're all in trouble.

The snow was brushing against the window in big, fat flakes, and we all bedded down and called it a night. We pushed some of the extra desks and chairs up against the walls to make some space to lie down. There'd been five wool blankets in the nurse's office, all folded into neat squares by the little doctor's office bed along the wall. The girls were sharing one. No one said much about it, just like no one said anything when Les and Elijah took two blankets and went back to the room on the other side of the hall.

Normally, anything even hinting at gayness would've been an endless source of jokes and abuse. Not now, though. We were homesick and cold and as bad as we had it, we knew others had it worse. I mean, there's no way all those buses made it to the end of their routes, for one thing. How'd you like to be stuck on a bus, buried up to its roof, on some little hillside road?

There was no way any of us guys were sharing a blanket, though. Jason agreed to go without tonight. He kept his jacket on and borrowed Pete's coat to put around his legs. Then he wrapped himself in about five of the sheets we'd also found in the nurse's office, along with the blankets, aspirin, bandages, and rubbing alcohol, which you could use for zits. Anyway, he said he'd be fine with the sheets.

I said, "Thanks," and he said, "Screw you, Weems." It was just our way of saying good night, I guess.

A Shinedown song came on. I sort of wanted to hear it, but someone got up and clicked off the radio, and that was fine too. Batteries.

Cell phone screens blinked on and then mostly right back off. We were starting to understand that it was something, you know, structural at this point, like all those dead spots on the radio dial. Pete played Alien Apokillypse for a while, but his battery was almost gone now. Some of the others had their earbuds in, but I couldn't hear whatever it was they were listening to. It was quiet, except for gusts of wind rattling the windows. An hour later, I was still awake. My side was sore from the tile floor, so I turned over. I didn't hear anyone else moving.

Then I did something I hadn't done for a very long time, probably not since I was a little boy. I prayed. I prayed for myself. I prayed for my mom. I prayed for all of us.

I guess maybe I felt a little self-conscious about it. I didn't get up and kneel or anything. I just curled up tight in the scratchy wool and whispered. Jason must've heard me, though. He was only a few feet away and he started to do the same thing. It's funny: It was probably the ten thousandth time I'd heard Jason say "Jesus," but it was the first time I'd heard him mean it.

Some people might have a problem with this. I mean, half of

them would be like, Prayer in a public school! We're not supposed to do that. Then the other half would think it was some sort of a deathbed conversion or whatever you want to call it. It's like, Oh, sure, *now* you're religious. Where was that on about fifty-one of the last fifty-two Sundays? And I don't know. I really don't. I'm not talking about our motives or our convictions or our lack of them. I'm just saying what happened. We prayed. We prayed for clear skies.

NINETEEN

The first thing I felt when I woke up Thursday morning was the cold. It's not that I was cold so much as that I knew it was cold around me. Have you ever left your window open overnight or anything like that and woken up with your room way too cold? It's weird because it actually makes it more comfortable to be curled up under the covers. Just knowing it's cold out there makes it feel better to be warm.

So there was some of that going on, but there's only so comfortable you're going to be after spending the night on a hard tile floor. And it wasn't a little cold in here. It wasn't leaving-your-window-open-in-April cold. It was wicked cold. The air was a sharp slap against the side of my face, waking me up, telling me that the last of the heat had drained away overnight.

I reached out from under the blanket and touched my cheek. My monster zit was bigger now, more tender, a little hill of sore flesh and pus pushing up through the side of my face. And there was one other thing bothering me: It might not sound like much, but I hadn't been online for like two solid days, and it was starting to freak me out.

The last time was Tuesday morning, before school, and that was just to answer some e-mails, respond to some comments, and play a few games: just the morning maintenance stuff. By now, I'd have a ton of e-mails and comments and posts. Everyone

167

would be checking in, seeing if I was OK, and stuff like that. Plus, my energy counter would be completely topped off in Mafia Wars—if I didn't use it, it wouldn't refill, which was just a huge waste—and my ship would be fixed by now in Scurvvy Piratez. I don't know why it bothered me so much. I guess when you're trying not to think too much about the big, real stuff, the little virtual stuff has to carry the load.

I heard a noise and looked over: Jason was picking through his stuff. He'd found one glove and was looking for the other. He hadn't seen me yet. I looked out the window. I guess I'd sort of been avoiding that, too. Pale gray light filtered in through the falling snow. You don't know that it's been snowing all night, I told myself. You're just making that assumption. But somehow I did know.

I remembered something that Andy had said on the radio late last night. "These things blow themselves out. They always have."

Of course, his voice was hoarse and he still hadn't had any good news to pass on when he said it, but I still found that kind of comforting.

I looked to the back of the room. I couldn't see Krista. The girls had pushed their backpacks and extra stuff into a little wall back there, like sandbags in a flood. I couldn't see them behind it, but I was pretty sure I heard whispering coming from that direction. They were awake but not up.

Without my phone, I wasn't exactly sure what time it was; around nine, if I had to guess. Why not sleep all day? What is there to do here, and what does it matter if we do it or not? I had to take a leak, though, and I wanted to take a good look at this zit, see if maybe it was ready to pop.

A sharp prickling sensation shot up my side as I got to my feet. It wasn't pain as much as feeling rushing back into the places the floor had crushed numb. The cold pushed in on me too, finding every little crack and bit of exposed skin. I reached down and grabbed my jacket. I saw one gloved hand sticking out from under Jason's little nest of sheets and coats. From the way it just hung there, I could tell he was already back to sleep.

Now that I was up, I could see Pete. He was lying just past Jason and staring up at the ceiling. I nodded to him, but he was a million miles away. I opened the classroom door as quietly as possible. When I touched the cold metal, I panicked for like half a second. I was thinking, Oh, man, what if my skin freezes to it? It wasn't nearly that cold, though, and I just pulled it closed behind me. I didn't have to worry about it clicking shut since we'd blown out the cylinder.

As I was making my way toward the men's room at the end of the hall, Les was making his way back. Our breath was visible in the air between us. We were like two steam trains heading toward each other on opposite tracks, like one of those word problems in algebra. When we were right next to each other, Les opened his spout and said: "Elijah says we're going to die in here."

So those were the first words I heard on our third day in the school.

"What?" I said. It's weird the effect words can have. These ones had stopped me cold.

"You heard me."

Fair enough, I had. I looked at him for a second, trying to process it.

"That's crazy," I finally managed. "It's been like two days. Well, two nights. And there's a ton of food in the caf. Like, literally, a ton."

"He didn't say we were going to starve," said Les, looking at me like I was impossibly dense. "He said we were going to die."

"It's still crazy," I said. And then, because he was still looking at me, and it was early, and I couldn't think of anything else, I said: "These things blow themselves out. They always have."

Les seemed to be considering that for a moment, maybe trying to remember where he'd heard it before. Then a little smile crept onto his face. "These things always blow," he said.

We both gave quick, snorting laughs and then went our separate ways, him back to the room on the other side of the hall and me to the zit-popping chamber. I was beginning to suspect that Les was OK. I just wasn't sure he should've been hanging out with Elijah.

It was even colder in the bathroom and, of course, there was no hot water. I still felt better when I left. I'd squeezed so much white pus out of the side of my face that my fingers had been slick with it. My cheek was bleeding a little but the pressure was gone. I stood in the hallway for a few moments, pressing the toilet paper to the side of my face.

I was thinking about what Les had said: We're going to die in here. I'd told him it sounded crazy, and it did, right? A thing like that? But I couldn't quite get it out of my head.

By the time I got back to the room, everyone was up. Again, why? But I wasn't one to talk. I'd been the first one on his feet. Anyway, the good thing about everyone being up was that they'd turned on the radio. I was glad for that. It sort of felt like there were more people when the radio was on. Jason was trolling the dial again — left glove on, right glove off — looking for other stations. Hopefully, there'd be something closer to home.

The Emergency Broadcasting Network still hadn't updated its message, and WKAR still hadn't dug itself out. A full trip around the dial later, and we were back to Andy. I figured he'd slept at the station, but I was wrong.

"Slept at the Hilton last night, folks," he was saying. "Not too shabby. Limited power and not much heat, but still not too shabby. A candlelit dinner with myself, the staff, and some very pissed-off business travelers. Very romantic . . ."

Apparently, the Hilton was connected to the office tower where the radio station was located. "I had to walk through a parking garage, but it's amazing the lengths I'll go to for some fresh frozen chicken," he said. "Even had some wine."

His voice sounded better and less ragged.

"Y'old dog," said Jason. We were all jealous. We wanted frozen chicken and hotel beds and limited power. They were basic things, but they were starting to sound like huge luxuries.

"Well, I think I've heard enough of this," said Pete. "I'm going back downstairs, maybe take another pass through the office."

He tossed a quick look over at Julie, but she wasn't biting. It was hard to flirt in this kind of cold. We weren't Eskimos.

Anyway, we let him go and started making guesses about how long he'd last before giving up.

"Fifteen minutes," said Jason.

"Twenty," said Julie. If she couldn't go with him, at least she could stick up for him a little. It was nice of her, I guess, but Jason knew Pete better and won the bet. Pete burst back into the room not quite ten minutes later. "It's pitch-black down there," he said, smacking his hands together, "and frickin' freezing!"

Pretty soon, Les and Elijah came in. It was pretty clear that they'd been laughing about something. Elijah looked like a little kid, bundled up in his jacket and sweater, with a smile just fading from his face. He was pale as bone, though, and I still remembered what Les said he'd told him.

I guess they'd heard the radio and headed across the hall. We had to have it up pretty high so we could still hear it as it faded in and out, and when they played a song, we never really bothered to turn it down.

With all of us in the same room, we had breakfast. We had these little plastic measuring cups we'd found in the kitchen area of the caf. Some of us used them for water and some of us used them as bowls for the peaches or pudding. There weren't enough cups to have one for each. We also used the same plastic spoons from the night before. Some of us had washed them out in the bathroom and some of us, not naming names, had just licked them clean.

Anyway, that was our breakfast: pudding and/or canned peaches and cold water in a cold room. The chocolate pudding was really thick. You sort of had to melt it with the heat from your mouth before swallowing. It wasn't bad, though, sort of like very rubbery ice cream.

I ate mine looking out the window. It looked like a cartoon world, everything out of proportion and wrong. The snow was maybe five feet below the window now, so it was, what, two feet below our feet? I wondered when this building had been built, a big stone monster, with ceilings fourteen feet high and a long way down from the second floor. It was a long way on a normal day, I mean. I could lower myself down now if I wanted to.

Farther out, the tops of trees looked like giant, frosted broccoli sprouts. The snow blew across the white field in front of us in little skittering waves. Nothing else moved.

Not much moved in the room either. We sat around bundled up, listening to the radio or talking or both. A few people still had their blankets over their shoulders. They sort of reminded me of those Revolutionary War soldiers in the history books, like: "Chapter 17, Valley Forge: A Test of Will."

Elijah went back to the room on the other side of the hall. Jason, Pete, and I were just sitting around and talking about random stuff: music, sports, things like that. The girls were too close for us to talk about them. It seemed like maybe they were talking about us, though. They had this way of talking low and close that meant they could be talking about anything, but there's no way we were going to do that. Lean into each other, almost touching foreheads, and whisper at 200 miles an hour? Please, we were dudes.

"Going down to the shop," Jason said after a while.

He stood up as he said it, so I had to tilt my head back to respond: "There light down there?"

"Yeah, it's like we thought. It's against that slope. No place for the snow to build up."

"Cool," I said.

Pete was no longer listening. His eyes had drifted to the back of the room again.

"Yeah, it's like sometimes the snow builds up, sort of drifts against the windows. But I just open and close 'em a few times hard and they clear right off. Still some frost, but the light comes in fine. It's really cold, but you warm up when you're working."

"Cool. How's the ol' *'werfer* coming along?"

"Good, good, I'm making a big change. I think you'll be surprised."

"I'll be surprised if it ever works!"

He brought his fist back and did a big, fake windmill windup, like in a cartoon. I bugged out my eyes and raised my hands and made an oh-no-don't-hit-me expression.

"Maybe I'll come down, help you out later?"

"Yeah, sure. If I'm not here, I'm there."

"Cool, cool."

"You gonna come too, Pete?" Jason said.

Pete swung his head back, not quite fast enough: "Huh?"

"Never mind, Romeo," Jason said, and he was gone.

About half an hour later, I got up and went back to the bathroom to pick the little scab of dried blood off my zit. It was good to have a mirror for that; you didn't want to get

174

it going again. I figured I'd put a little more Oxy on there too. With the really big ones, it's important to kick 'em while they're down.

So anyway, I did that and bent down to wash my hands. I turned the faucet knob and nothing came out. At first I thought I'd turned the wrong one. The water had been weak in here earlier, and I figured it was because there was no hot water with the heat and electricity out. But I looked again and saw the little C pressed into the metal. I turned it all the way on and still nothing.

"Aw, man," I said, straightening up and talking to my face in the mirror.

I walked over to the closest urinal and pushed the lever down: nothing. I walked back to the room. Everyone looked over when I came in, just like everyone looked over anytime anyone came in. We were light on entertainment. "One of you girls want to go try the faucets in the girls' room?" I said while I had their attention.

"Why?" said Krista.

" 'Cause there's no water in the men's room."

"Pipes freeze?" said Les, sitting near the radio.

"There could just be no pressure," said Pete. He was disagreeing just to disagree. You could tell there was some real tension building between those two. I think it had started with their little showdown outside the nurse's office, but it might have been before that.

"I don't know why," I said. "All I know is that there's no water, alright?"

"This sucks!" said Julie, getting to her feet.

Pete made a little move as she approached the door.

"What?" said Les. "You gonna go to the john with her too?"

Pete glared back at him but settled back into his chair.

"Oh, yeah," I said as she passed me on her way out the door. "I wouldn't use the toilet if I were you."

She reappeared a minute later: "Nothing."

This was bad. People stood up and started pacing and complaining. I guess Elijah heard us, because he reappeared from across the hall. He glided silently into the room with the gray blanket trailing behind him like a cape. He took a seat next to Les and gave him a little look, like, What's up?

"No water," said Les, filling him in. "And we can't flush the toilets."

Elijah smiled a little. I don't think he was enjoying our misfortune. I think he'd just seen it coming. We were all watching him now, and he knew it. His little bone-white hand appeared from beneath the blanket and floated outward until it was pointing at the windowsill.

"Aw, you're kidding me!" said Krista.

Les walked over and picked up what Elijah had been pointing at: the nearly empty pudding can.

"They don't call it 'going to the can' for nothing," Elijah said. "And then you just dump it out the window."

Les handed it to him, and he held it out for us to see. Why did it have to be the chocolate pudding?

"Alright," said Krista, rolling her eyes, "but . . . just . . . ugh!"

"We'll need one for water too," said Pete. "To melt snow to make water."

"Yeah, we *cannot* use the same one for that!" said Julie.

Les walked back over and picked up the peaches. That one was more than half full, though. "Well," he said, "looks like we'll need some more cans."

"It'll take forever for the snow to melt in here," I said, pushing out a long spout of white breath.

"We'll need to build a fire," said Elijah.

It was something we'd avoided. It just hadn't seemed like a good idea. There was no ventilation in here, no fireplace, and nowhere to run if things got out of control. And wasn't Elijah the one who'd said we were all going to die in here? What was he trying to do, make sure he was right?

"Man," I said. "I don't know."

I was alone, though. Everyone else really liked the idea.

"What d'ya mean, man?" Pete said. "We need to melt the water, and it'll be warm, man. Nice and warm."

That sealed the deal. And anyway, I didn't want to fall back into the super-cautious Ned Flanders role I'd had the first two days: "Should we really?" "Will we get in trouble?" I was a little embarrassed by all that now.

"Alright," I said, "but we'll need a separate room where we can keep a window cracked."

"No problema," said Les, eager to break another lock.

"And we'll need something better than a peach can for it," I continued. "And some way to start it and stop it quick."

And that's how I ended up on my way down to visit Jason in the shop a few hours before I'd planned. I had both hands on the railing as I headed down into the dark stairwell. Fire Marshall Weems reporting for duty.

TWENTY

"A fire?" Jason was saying. "Are you sure that's a good idea?"

It had taken me a good fifteen minutes to get to the shop, feeling my way along the walls and lockers like a mole in ski gloves. The air was cold and tight and I was breathing harder than I should've been by the time I pushed open the busted door on the industrial arts room. The air was better in there because of all that opening and closing of the windows, I guess.

"No," I answered, "but they're all pretty set on it."

"Mmmm," he said as he leaned in to tighten a bolt with a monkey wrench. I wasn't sure if that was a response or a grunt.

"Anyway, we've got to melt the snow somehow," I continued, "and a room with some heat wouldn't be such a bad thing."

"No," he said, putting the wrench down and looking up. "But burning the school down would."

"I'll give you that," I said, grinning like an idiot. The over-sized goggles he was wearing made him look like a bug, and safety lectures from bugs are hard to take seriously.

"I'll tell you what," he went on, ignoring me. "That room would heat up nicely if we got some sun. Those two big windows . . . Then the snow would melt quick enough. You know how hot it gets in here."

He waved his work glove at the wall of windows at the back of the room. He was right about that. It got hot as balls in here, especially when you had all the safety gear on and were leaning into a belt sander.

"Yeah, dude, but we'd be out of here if we got some sun. All we're getting is more snow, so I think, you know, we have to think about that."

"Yeah," he said. "I guess that's true. I heard there was a nor'easter that lasted, like, a week. In the '60s or something."

I sort of wondered where he'd "heard" this, and why he'd been keeping it to himself.

"Probably lasted a day," I said. "Those people were so stoned."

We both laughed. I was in a strange mood, not good exactly but not as bad as you'd think. The prevailing atmosphere of DOOM was making me a little punchy. It was nice to be out of that room for a while, in any case, so I figured I'd stretch it out a bit.

"Man, whatcha doin' with this thing?" I said, nodding toward the *Flammenwerfer*. It was looking a lot different than the last time I'd seen it.

"You really want to know?" he said. From the big smile breaking out on his face, I could tell he was going to tell me anyway. "I'm turning it into a snowmobile!"

"Seriously?"

"Yeah, it'll totally work better that way. Check it out—"

He was walking to the back of the kart to show me something, but as soon as I realized he was serious I cut him off.

"That's dumb, man. You heard the radio. We're supposed to stay put."

"For how long? You're the one who said 'All we're getting is more snow.' Anyway," he said, shrugging, "I didn't say I was going to use it. It just, you know, gives me something to do . . . other than sitting around watching Pete make moonie faces at Julie. Ugh."

"Yeah, can't argue with that," I said. I was secretly glad he hadn't mentioned the moonie faces I'd been making at Krista.

"Anyway, check it out. You know how I was having problems getting the driveshaft to work? Without, you know, spraying the room with shrapnel?"

Not to get too technical about it, but that had been the big problem with the kart so far. The engine was just a big lawn mower engine, so it had one shaft that spun straight underneath it. But the wheels were on both sides, not straight underneath. So he had to find some way to hook the engine up to the wheels. At first, he'd tried this heavy-duty bike chain hookup, but it had come apart at high revs and nearly killed Pete. Missed him by like a foot. So then he'd moved on to this "rotating coupling" thing, like on a real car, but that was super complicated. And, to be honest, it was probably more dangerous than the bike chain.

"Yeah," I said.

"Well, I don't even need to do it on this. I can just tilt the engine down so the shaft is pointing out the back and hook a propeller right to it."

"Like, you mean, like those airboats they use in the Everglades?"

"Yeah, yeah, just like that! And instead of wheels, I'll just make the bottom like a sled. Super simple!"

"Dude, man, that's pretty cool."

"Thanks. It's a lot easier too. It's not a go-kart." He paused, smiling. "It's a snow-kart! I think it might work."

"Yeah, I'm pretty sure you'd break your neck if you actually used it. But you might get an A out of it."

"You think?"

"Totally."

He'd definitely get an A. "Stranded Kid Builds Propeller Sled." How do you not get an A for that?

"Cool, it'll be my legacy. They'll find its charred remains after we burn down the school."

"Yeah, they'll probably award you the Nobel Prize and stuff," I said. Then, because I still couldn't get it out of my head, I added, "Elijah says we're all going to die in here."

Jason looked at me and snorted: "He would."

That made me feel better, the way he just blew it off like that.

TWENTY-ONE

"We've got all the fixin's, folks," said Jason, kicking open the door to the main room.

It hadn't been easy to haul all of this stuff back from shop. Our arms were full of pretty much everything we needed to set up a good, safe, and relatively small fire. At least we hoped it would be small.

Between us we had a blowtorch, sparker, fire extinguisher, empty paint cans, an old metal bucket half full of sand, and some 2x4s. We figured we'd start off by burning some clean wood before we started breaking up the furniture. We dumped the stuff in a heap by the door and stood there, leaning forward with our hands on our knees, breathing hard. The frost plumes of our breath pushed halfway across the room before disappearing.

"What, are you gonna build it right there?" asked Pete.

"No, you idiot," said Jason. Pete was in his doghouse for staying up here with the girls instead of coming down and checking out his snow-kart, and for not helping us carry this stuff. "I just thought I'd get some feeling back in my shoulders for a second."

Pete didn't say anything. I think he kind of knew what was going on. Julie, not so much.

"Where should we build it?" she said.

Everyone was waiting for Jason to answer, and he kept them waiting for a few long moments. No one even looked at me.

"Need a new room," he said finally, straightening up and rolling his shoulders.

"Why?" said Julie.

"Because," he said, and for a second it seemed like that was all he was going to say. He seemed annoyed to be having this discussion. Finally, he added: "Well, for one thing, we'll need to leave a window open."

"For ventilation?" I said. I was like his dopey helper, asking him simple questions. I knew he wouldn't necessarily explain things otherwise.

"Yeah," he said, turning to me with a little smirk. He knew what I was doing, and that I'd probably keep doing it, so he explained everything nice and slow.

"Yeah, I mean, I think you guys might think this little fire is going to bring warmth back into our Happy Home, but mostly it's just going to bring fire into it. We'll have to crack a window above it, for ventilation and to give it enough oxygen. But an open window isn't like a chimney. The smoke won't just magically climb out, so the room is going to be seriously smoky anyway. And the window will let in more cold than the fire produces heat."

"Well, that all sucks," said Krista. She sounded legitimately sad about it, and Jason relented a little.

"Well, it will melt the snow quick enough, and if you're sitting right by it, it'll be warm. Plus, we can use it to, like, heat up our gloves and blankets and stuff. So that'll, you know . . ."

Jason couldn't bring himself to say "be nice," so he just waved one hand around in a circular way that he probably considered the outer limits of girlishness and everyone got the idea. A big gust of wind rattled the windows, and Jason went on.

"And we should pick a room on the other side of the hall, facing the courtyard. There's way too much wind out there to open a window facing the front. The smoke'll never get out and we don't want a sudden burst of oxygen like that around the fire either."

So I was looking at Jason giving his little fire-safety lecture and I started picturing him in one of those red plastic fire hats. He looked over at the end and I had that same stupid grin on my face as before, like I was just about to start laughing. It was at least the third or fourth time since this started that he'd caught me acting like an idiot.

"This is serious, Weems," he said. "Moron."

So basically he let me off easy.

We picked the room right across the hall, just next to the one Elijah and Les had staked out. There were pros and cons to this. Pro: It was close to both rooms, and we could keep an eye on it. Con: It was close to both rooms, and a fire in a bucket in the middle of a tile floor seemed like it could get out of hand pretty quickly. I'd heard that this kind of tile burned better than wood once it got going.

Jason's thinking was that if the fire got out of control we were all going to die, regardless of where it started. It was probably true, but again, not too comforting.

We also designated that room as our new bathroom. It was unisex: We were, like, true progressives. You went in there, pulled the blind down on the door, and did your business right in front of the fire. Then you dumped it out the already open window into fifteen or sixteen feet of snow, swished a little water around in the can, and left it for the next customer.

It was a good plan because the bathrooms had been getting a little too cold even before the pipes froze. It had been like instant open-air shrinkage. Plus, it guaranteed that there'd be a steady stream of people into the room, to keep an eye on the fire and feed it more wood now and then.

The fire was just a little pyramid of broken-up chunks of 2x4s to begin with, stacked neatly on top of the sand in the old metal bucket.

"Like a cookout on a beach," Jason said.

The sand was originally meant to throw on chemical fires in the shop, but it was also good at keeping the bottom of the bucket from getting too hot against the floor.

So we started with the 2x4s, but after a while, any wood would do. If you want to know a secret, textbooks were even better. The big ones burned slow, like Yule logs. We had the blowtorch and sparker, so it was no big deal to start it up. And we kept the fire extinguisher by the door. It seemed like a pretty slick plan all around.

By afternoon, the commode situation was sorted out and our little fire bucket was working fine. We were all back in the main room together and, well, you could kind of smell it. Even in the cold, we were starting to smell and feel a little funky. I'd had the same socks and underwear on since Tuesday morning. My hair felt oily, itchy, and gross under my hat. No one really took their hats off anymore. And looking around, I could see that I wasn't the only one having acne trouble.

Anyway, by the time the smell of smoke started creeping under the door, I think we were all a little glad. It did a decent job of covering up our funk. And the fire wasn't out of control or anything. It seemed small and harmless in its little bucket. It was just that it was too windy, even out in the courtyard, for the smoke to make its way out the window without a lot of detours. The thick, oily smoke from the burning lumber seemed almost curious, the way it crept under every door and into every corner. And if you closed your eyes, you could almost imagine a fireplace crackling away somewhere nearby.

TWENTY-TWO

So our little fire-in-a-bucket was working pretty well, and I've got to say, the hits just kept on coming. That afternoon, for the first time since the storm had started, the snow really slowed down. It didn't quite stop, but it let up enough so that you really noticed. Just a quick look out the window and you could see it was different.

And so, of course, that's what we were doing. We were staring out the window, all of us except for Jason, who'd gone back down to the shop. It was around three o'clock. We were getting down to the last of our cafeteria supplies and were talking about who should go back for more and if maybe we could make a torch or something for the trip. The emergency lights hadn't come back on, and we were kind of on a fire kick anyway.

"Look at the snow," Julie had said. It sounded like a tremendously stupid statement, considering that it had been snowing for days and we were almost buried in the stuff, so most of us didn't look over. But Pete did, of course.

"Wow," he said, and then everyone looked.

Now we were sitting in our chairs or standing by the window and watching. I was thinking: This is just a normal snowfall. It looked like snow in all of those old movies, just some fluffy flakes drifting lazily to the ground while some crooner is singing in the background and everyone is dreaming of a white Christmas or going to grandma's house or whatever.

How many snowfalls just like this had I seen in my life: dozens, hundreds? It wasn't the foot-an-hour whiteout that had shut everything down on Tuesday, or even the hard, driving snow that had kept it shut down since then. It was just snowing. The only thing remarkable about it now was that it still hadn't stopped for three days.

With the snow so much lighter, it seemed like maybe the cell phones might have a shot. Everyone tried and got nothing, but then Pete had the bright idea to open the window and, like, lean out. It was kind of a shot in the dark, but his phone was basically out of battery power at that point — too low for his game or his flashlight app — so it was like a last hurrah.

The wind had died down, along with the snow, so it was cold when the two of us wrestled the heavy window open, but there was no blast of arctic air or anything like that. Pete brushed away the mini-snowbank on the sill and leaned out into the open air with his elbows on the frame and his phone out in front of him.

"Anything?" said Julie.

Pete had this look of intense concentration on his face, like he was trying to communicate with ESP instead of AT&T. "Nah," he said. "Nuh-uh."

Then he leaned out a little farther and held his phone up above his head.

"Careful," said Julie.

"Watch it," I said.

It was mostly calm, like I said, but every now and then a little gust of wind would whip sideways across the front of the school. There was another one right then. It wasn't big or anything, but it must've blown some snow into Pete's eye or something like that.

"Son of a . . ." he said, reaching back toward his face with his left hand.

The phone was still out there in his right hand, just on his fingertips, and then it wasn't. We all watched as it tipped and fell. I leaned forward and ducked my head out the open window just in time to see it hit the snow. It dug in a few inches, but you could still see it in there, just this faint glow rising up through the snow.

"Oh, crap!" said Pete.

I made the snap decision not to bust on him about it. Les made the opposite decision, but Pete wasn't really listening. He was just looking down at the little glowing line in the snow, not all that far below the window now but too far to reach. After that, there was nothing to do but shut the window before the room got too cold. It closed with a heavy thud. So long, little flashlight, I thought. It had been worth a shot.

After that, we just went back to what we were doing. I was standing there with a blanket wrapped around me, watching this seen-it-a-thousand-times-before snow as if it was some fascinating new phenomenon. And that's when I saw it. At first, it was just a shape, something dark moving behind the shifting patterns of the fat white flakes. I thought maybe it was a bird, but it was too far away. It was too far away, and that meant that

197

it was too big. It was too far away and too big and too metallic. And then it must have turned toward us because I could see its light.

"Does anyone . . . Do you see?" I said. "It's a helicopter!"

It made this big sweeping turn in the air, flew a little closer, and then moved steadily away. It didn't really come all that close to us. It was hard to gauge distance with all that altitude between us, but I guessed it was maybe a half a mile away. So it wasn't exactly a flyover. We couldn't hear its rotors or anything, but it was close enough so that we could see that it was dark green. It was military.

I was thinking, Man, Jason's going to be mad he missed this, and right then he burst through the door. "There was . . . Did you see?" he huffed. "There was a helicopter!"

It's funny, because that's almost exactly what I'd said. But how did he know about it? The shop was on the other side of the building. What, had he used his MSP: military sensory perception?

"It just swung around over the river and then I lost sight of it," he said.

"Oh, man," I said. "It, like, circled the building!"

"Yeah?" he said. "How close did it come on this side?"

"Maybe like half a mile."

"Yeah, it was about the same on the other."

"Do you think it saw us?" said Julie as if the helicopter was some sort of creature.

"They don't need to see us," said Les. "They know we're here."

I hoped that was true, and I felt a little embarrassed that I'd waved my arms as it flew by, half a mile away. I wasn't the only one, though.

Anyway, that was downright exciting. We all stayed there for a while, even Jason, chattering about it and what it meant. We all thought that maybe this was it. The storm was winding down and pretty soon everything would be running again and we'd be out of here.

Les and Elijah went back to their room so they could keep an eye out from that side of the building. Jason went back down to the shop, and some of us came and went from the fire room, and then at some point I looked up and it was just Krista and me in the main room. Pete and Julie were gone. There's no chance Pete would go into the other room with Les, and I hadn't seen them when I'd gone to take a leak.

I looked over at Krista. All of a sudden I was nervous again.

"Uh?" I said. It wasn't much, but she knew what I meant.

She just put her finger up to her lips and made a small shushing sound. So she knew they'd slipped off together. Pete had just snuck out on me, but I guess Julie must've told Krista. Chicks always talked more about that stuff than guys.

I was thinking: Where are they, back stairwell? I looked across the floor, and sure enough, Pete had taken his blanket. That dog!

I looked back over at Krista. None of this was news to her. She was looking down at her book again. She was reading *The Great Gatsby*, which is a really small, thin book, and she was trying to turn the page with her big ski gloves. It took her like three tries and she had this look of total concentration on her face the whole time. Her knees were pulled up to her chest and her feet were crossed. She was wearing these little white slip-on sneakers.

I was staring, but I sort of couldn't help it. It's like my muscles weren't responding. The look on her face, the way her feet were crossed, just everything . . . Make fun of me if you want, but it was the most beautiful thing I'd ever seen. I was lost in it.

Did you ever go to the beach when you were a little kid and get wiped out by a wave? You know how you get tumbled around down there and come up spitting saltwater? You're dizzy and disoriented and all you can do is try to stand up, even though you know another wave might hit you any second? Well, that's pretty much how I felt right then. I wasn't spitting water, though, at least not much.

I was thinking: Is this what love is, feeling like you've been spun around underwater? Forgetting how cold you are, until she looks up and you look down and you're embarrassed and the world comes rushing back in? Or is love not being able to get that image out of your head, the image of the moment right before she looked up?

Or was I just being an idiot? When her head had started to come up, I'd assumed she was looking up at me, but I was wrong. She was looking out the window. It was something she'd seen out of the corner of her eye.

"Oh, no," she said softly.

I looked over. It was really coming down again.

TWENTY-THREE

Within an hour it was snowing full force again, as if someone was up on the roof pushing it off by the shovelful. The daylight lasted just long enough for us to get a good look at this truly depressing sight. Everyone was back in the room, listening to the radio, and the mood had taken a nosedive.

Pete gave Jason and me this ridiculous excuse about how he'd tried to go to the shop to see the snow-kart but had gotten lost in the dark. So lame: The school wasn't *that* big. We didn't really push him on it, though. It didn't seem like the time for it, with the storm back to full strength and everyone close together in the same room.

Listen, it's not like I cared all that much what base Pete did or did not get to, out there on the stairs or wherever they were. It just kind of bothered me that he didn't feel like he could tell his friends about it.

Anyway, right now, we were listening to Elijah. Will wonders never cease, right? He'd been talking to Les, and Les had been laughing, so Jason was like, "What's so funny?"

We didn't have a lot of entertainment options in our little room, and anything that'd take our minds off the cold was welcome. So now we were all facing Elijah, or his shadow, anyway. The sun had gone down and that was all you could see of anyone. We'd gotten pretty good at identifying people by their shapes. It was the hoods, hats, and jackets that gave us away, since we'd been wearing the same outfits for days.

Elijah was talking about the time Georgie Tate had put his head through the sheetrock dividing wall in the library. We'd all heard about it, but Elijah was one of the few people who'd seen it happen. Like I said, he was always in the library.

He was saying that it wasn't in a fight, like everyone thought. He hadn't bull rushed Joe Sindelar and missed. Elijah was saying how it was a dare, and how Georgie was only mad at Joe afterwards.

It was a pretty funny story, actually. I guess you sort of have to know Georgie, who's a nice enough guy but way too excitable. Anyway, the dare was to ram his head into the wall while the librarian was out of the room, and it just didn't occur to him that he might end up putting his head right through the sheetrock.

So now we all knew the truth of what happened and we got to have a few last laughs at Georgie's expense, and it was all thanks to Elijah. It was the first time he'd really spoken up much in the room. Mostly, he made little comments on the side to Les, and Les would make that little clucking laugh of his.

I'd assumed he was laughing because Elijah had said something weird or morbid or whatever, and that that's why Les liked him. Now it occurred to me that maybe he was laughing because Elijah was actually kind of funny, nothing more complicated than that.

So anyway, we ended the day laughing, and that was fitting. The day hadn't been all that bad. I mean, yeah, there was the whole crapping-in-a-pudding-can thing, and it was nearly as cold inside as out now, but there'd been encouraging things too. A helicopter flew by the school — a "rescue chopper" Jason had called it — and the storm had let up for a while.

As decent as the day had been, it was a drag to bed down for another cold night on the hard floor. All of us were in here now, because it was too cold for Elijah and Les to stay across the hall. Our only heat sources were body heat and the hot air from any talking we might do. It wasn't much against the whole outside, gone mad with winter. If you got too cold, you could go and sit in front of the fire bucket, but you had to sit right in front of it. That room was below freezing with the window open.

It wasn't even seven o'clock, but it had been dark for a while. We'd just eaten the last scraps of food and would need to go back to the caf tomorrow. Now there was nothing to do except hunker down and listen to the radio. We'd all built little nests with our jackets and blankets and anything else we could find. Julie turned the radio up so we could all hear without leaving our nests.

The little window in the storm was passing over Hartford now. Andy was excited about it. He was looking out the window, and he could see some people moving around downtown with flashlights and camping lanterns. One guy even had a home-made torch, like a caveman in the city.

It was sort of fun to hear about. People were moving around and going outside for the first time in days. But those people didn't know that the storm wasn't over. I just hoped they didn't wander too far into it.

A while later, we turned off the radio to save batteries. There was nothing to do but hope for sleep. Of course, another word for hope is pray, and that was something we could do too. Jason and I got up out of our nests. He'd found another blanket in a cupboard in the shop. It was made to throw over chemical fires and not for comfort, but it was better than relying on a bunch of sheets to stay warm. I'm not sure of my point here, except that it was a proper nest he was climbing out of.

Anyway, we kneeled there on the floor and prayed. Not loud, but enough so that we could hear each other.

"Gimme a break," said Pete, tossing a book at us. "Bible thumpers!"

He was kidding. All he meant was that he wouldn't be joining us, and that was fine. Jason went first, and he was halfway through when someone came up and joined us. I knew it was one of the girls, but it took me a while to figure out that it was Krista. It's funny how you can recognize someone's voice in how they cry. She was just crying a little, just small, soft sobs, and she got it under control once she knelt down.

I guess, if you think about it, church was probably something she did with her family. Now she didn't know how much of her family was left. Same for Jason. I'm amazed we weren't all crying, though I bet if you woke up in the night, you'd hear others.

Anyway, when it was my turn, I prayed to the archangel Gabriel. He's the one with the trumpet, the one that made the announcements. That's what we wanted, right? We wanted news. It didn't have to be divine, just good.

The whole thing probably didn't last more than three or four minutes. Then we climbed back into our nests. Maybe we slept better, maybe we didn't. I will say this: I only woke up once during the night. It was something I heard: a deep rumbling sound.

At first I thought it was thunder, but that was impossible. It doesn't thunder during snowstorms, right? I was groggy and it was the middle of the night, so when I didn't hear it again, I sort of wondered if I'd ever heard it in the first place. The mind plays tricks, you know? I guess if I'd thought about it more, I might've figured it out. But a few minutes later, I fell back to sleep.

TWENTY-FOUR

It was still snowing the next morning. Of course it was. This would be our fourth straight day in the school and, without a doubt, the worst one yet. I didn't know it at the time, but I guess I got a clue when I woke up to the sound of someone sneezing.

I was too sleepy to figure out where the sneeze had come from, but it didn't really matter. Some kind of bug had been lingering in someone's system, and after all these days of cold temps, crappy food, and not much in the way of sanitation, it'd pushed its way back to the surface. Soon, we'd all have it. How could we not? We were all living in the same room, windows closed.

I climbed out from under my blanket. No need to put my jacket back on. I hadn't used it as a pillow the way I had the first few nights up here: I'd worn it. But still, the cold hit me as soon as I stood up, pricking my face and my fingers as I pulled on my sneakers and tied them. If I had to guess, I'd say the temperature was down to forty degrees in the main room now, and colder in the hallways. I put my gloves back on, straightened my hat, and went to the bucket room.

A wave of dark smoke hit me as I pushed the door open. For a second, I panicked, thinking maybe the bucket had tipped over and the whole room was on fire. But it was just a little smoke pushing out into the open air of the hallway. When I got closer,

I could see that the fire was almost out. I pulled a chair up in front of it, took my gloves off, and spent maybe five minutes getting it going again.

I added some of the paper we'd stacked under a brick nearby: notebook paper, old tests, stuff like that. Then I threw in a few more chunks of 2x4 and waited for it to catch. I was in no hurry, the warmth felt good on my fingers. Once it got going, I leaned down and let it warm my face. I took my hat off and pushed my fingers back through my greasy hair.

I stood up and held the old pudding can in my left hand as I took a leak. Then I walked over to the open window and dumped it out. I looked down at the first stain of the day, a golden-yellow hole melted in the surface of the snow. The other, darker stains from yesterday were totally covered now. It was like the storm didn't want to look at them anymore either.

It would've seemed impossible, even just a few days ago, but the snow was maybe three feet below the second-floor window-sill. I looked out. How long would it take to reach the windows? It was already drifting up against some of them. Could it keep going long enough to cover them, like it'd covered the ones downstairs? There was no higher ground, no place left for us to go.

It was early and my mind was still muddy and unclear. I sort of let it stay that way. There are times when you want to think clearly, and I just felt like this was not one of them. Thinking clearly would just make me more aware of how screwed we were, more aware that there was nothing one fifteen-year-old could do to stop a storm.

As it was, I was thinking about how my season was going down the drain. Our first game had been canceled and our second game was supposed to be tomorrow night. I felt weak right down to my joints. I went through the motions of a jump shot, imagining the basket along the far wall. Normally, I picture those going in, but this one felt offline, maybe even short. I could almost hear Coach now: "Basket's that way, Weems!" I wondered if there was any way to practice in a dark gym.

There was still no one knocking on the door or tapping at the glass for their turn, so I sat back down and had a drink from the water cup. I remembered the sneeze I'd heard. Next time, I'd bring my own cup.

We'd refilled the jumbo-sized peach can with snow from the windowsills three or four times now, but you could still taste the peach syrup that used to be in it. And it was warm too, because we kept it near the fire to melt. It was like warm peach water, kind of good, actually. I downed the first cup and had a second.

It turned out there had been someone waiting. It's just that Elijah was not the type to knock. He'd just been waiting silently. For how long, I wondered. Had he seen the jump shot? Could he tell it was a miss?

I'd kept him waiting long enough, and I knew he probably had to take a leak. But it was the first time I'd seen him alone in days, and there was something I had to ask him.

"What did you mean, we're all going to die here?" I said. "That goth crap is just not cool. Not now."

It came out more hostile than I'd intended. Again, it was early. Elijah took a moment to process it and then fired back.

"I'm not goth," he said, blinking into the light coming from the open door. "Is that what you think this is, me trying to be dark and cool and morbid, pretending to be a vampire or something stupid like that? I know this is serious, and I guess maybe I shouldn't have said that to Les. I didn't mean it literally. It was just, 'We're gonna frickin' die,' like, we're all screwed, you know? And we are."

Now my mind was the one struggling to process all those words, so I just asked him about that last part.

"Yeah, why's that?" I said. It was a truly stupid question: Why were we screwed? Why weren't we, was more like it. At least I tried to dial my tone back a bit.

"They don't know we're here," he said.

"Who doesn't?" I said, but I must've known. I must've, because the words hit me hard in the stomach.

"They think we were on the buses. You know some of them didn't make it. And if they did, people will just think we didn't make it home from the bus stop. Even if they know we were getting picked up, they'll just assume we got picked up and never made it. And our phones might as well be bricks."

"Jason's dad knows," I said. "Krista's mom . . ."

"Are you dense? They were both on the road. So was my . . . Anyway, you can't even see the road now. Can't even see where it used to be. We're missing, and so are they, probably. How many people do you think are missing right now?"

"Yeah," I said. "What about Gossell?"

He just looked at me, and I looked down at my feet. It was getting a little late in the game to believe in fairy tales.

"No one knows we're here," he said finally. It didn't sound weird or morbid or anything. It just sounded like a fact.

TWENTY-FIVE

By the time I got back to the room, Jason was already up. He had half a cup of water left from last night and was brushing his teeth with his finger. I should probably do that too, I thought. The girls might've had some toothpaste left, but I doubted they'd share. Jason had his hat and jacket on and was getting ready to go to the shop.

Across the room, Julie sneezed. So she was the one who had brought the snot into our little world. I left the room a minute later, tagging along with Jason. I knew it wouldn't matter much. Within a day or two, we'd all have Julie's bug, starting with Pete.

You know that phrase, "I could do that with my eyes closed"? Well, that was a pretty good description of Jason making the trip to the shop. It was pitch-dark by the time we reached the bottom of the stairwell, but he barely even slowed down. He was talking to me, but it wasn't to talk, it was to let me know where he was, which way to go.

We were moving too fast. It felt lame to say so, so I didn't. I kept one hand along the wall and did my best to keep up. Still, I mean, what was the hurry? We had only two things in this world: snow and time. And all it would take was a pen on the floor for me to fall and break my wrist or something. And wouldn't that just cap off a magical week?

A few minutes later, we were at the back of the school, and weak light was leaking out into the hallway through the broken glass of the shop room's door. Jason pushed it open. He went to the back windows to slam some of the snow off, then went right to the big table where his snow-kart was lying upside down. I got the impression that he knew exactly where he'd left off and what he wanted to do next.

For a kid obsessed with war and stuck in what was basically becoming an underground bunker, this was good for Jason. It was something to keep him occupied, something to do. I left him to it: I had my own project in mind.

There's this thing, I guess you'd call it a theory. It's called Occam's razor. The first time I heard it mentioned, I thought it was Ockham's racer, which is why I paid attention. There's this NASCAR driver named Jeremy Ockham and, whatever, it's an easy mistake to make. Anyway, the theory is just that the simplest solution is usually the best one. It's not like I needed some ancient dude to come up with a theory to tell me that, but that's the way the world works: First one in gets the prize.

Anyway, Jason's snow-kart was a lot simpler than it had been. Just switching out four wheels for one propeller made it simpler. But it still had a lot of moving parts, and that meant a lot of things could still go wrong. I figured I'd make something simpler. Really, they were just about the simplest things you could think of. And sure enough, I was almost done by lunchtime.

I left Jason down there, still working, and went back up. I say lunchtime but we really didn't have any food left, except for some peanut butter and jelly with no bread, so we had to plan the next trip to the cafeteria. When I got back into the main room, they were already talking about it. It's like they were drawing straws.

"Maybe you and Weems should go," Les was saying to Krista.

"No way," said Krista. "We did our part."

"Yeah, but you, like, know where stuff is," said Les.

"Not really," she said. "It was pretty dark then and it will be totally dark now. I wouldn't even know which way was up."

This is maybe lame to admit, but it kind of hurt my feelings. That first trip to the caf with Krista had been like the one highlight of this whole thing. I even thought, maybe . . . Well, whatever, it just kind of sucked that she didn't want to do it again. I heard myself saying that I didn't want to go either. It was like, you can't fire me, I quit.

It didn't matter much: Pete and Julie were happy to make the trip. No surprise there.

"Try to be back before dinner," Les said with a smirk.

Julie laughed, but Pete shot Les a look. Pete needed to be careful with that. I made a mental note to mention it to him when he got back.

The trip wasn't exactly going to be a tunnel of love, though. It was permanent midnight down there, and there were enough things to run into or trip over to make it legitimately dangerous.

We had a long talk about making a torch or something like that. I won't bore you with the details because we didn't do it. They just took Krista's iPhone and used the little bit of light from that. It was really all the things were good for at that point, except to drive us crazy.

During the "War and Its Aftermath" section in U.S. history, we learned about "phantom limb syndrome," where people have a limb amputated or whatever but the nerve endings are still attached so sometimes it's like they can still feel it, like maybe they have an itch in their missing leg. That's what it was like to be without working cell phones for so long. Sometimes I'd go to check mine, only to remember it was still home on the dresser. And thinking of home just made me worry about my mom again.

And it wasn't any better for the others. I'd see Jason just sitting there for like fifteen minutes at a time, watching the little picture of an envelope for his text message flip over and over, not disappearing, not being sent. When the screen timed out and went black, he flicked it back on and went back to watching the little envelope. So it was like phantom cell phone syndrome. In a way, it was really stupid, but it seemed just as real as the cold.

Anyway, Pete and Julie came back sooner than expected. I guess maybe it was too cold down there for much fooling around. Pete was saying how the iPhone worked pretty well: "It's not much help in the hallways, but you can bring it right into the walk-in fridge and hold it up to the labels."

Krista and I had done the same thing, of course, and the similarities didn't end there. "Uh, dude," I said, "you brought back, like, the exact same things we did."

And it was true. They'd dumped their haul out in the center of the room: PB&J, bread, cold cuts, pudding, peaches . . .

"And cookies!" said Julie, holding up a jumbo pack of fake

Oreos and sounding a little defensive. "You guys didn't find the cookies."

"Well," I said, "I guess that's something."

"Fine," said Julie. "We'll go back down."

No one protested too loudly. We were sick of pudding and peaches.

They'd been gone maybe two minutes when I heard that weird sound again: *RRRRMMM!* It was like two tons of gravel shifting around above our heads. This time I knew it wasn't thunder, and I knew I wasn't dreaming or imagining it, because we all heard it.

"What the — ?" said Les.

"I don't like the sound of that," said Krista.

I gave Elijah a quick look: We could always count on him for the bad news.

"It's the snow," he said. "Pressing down on the roof."

TWENTY-SIX

We pawed through the fresh supplies. It was just Krista, Elijah, Les, and me in the room. Four days ago, I would've said this was the weirdest collection of students you could imagine. What did any of us have in common?

Krista was one of the school's few truly hot girls. What were there, maybe a dozen, total? She was a freshman but she could talk to the juniors and seniors like she was one of them. I'd seen her do it. She could go anywhere in the school. She could talk to whoever she wanted and she could ignore whoever she wanted. Being good-looking, it was like a passport to anywhere, and she was the only one of us who had one.

As for Elijah, like I said, most people associated him with the goth kids, but he wasn't really part of that scene. I used to just think he was spooky, but the truth is, I'd never really had to think about him all that much. All I knew was how he looked, where he hung out, and things like that. And when he was one of hundreds of kids I was passing in the hallways five days a week, that seemed like all I needed to know. The popular kids called him names or just ignored him.

No one called Les names. Not to his face. All I knew about him was that he was always getting in trouble. If there was such a thing as permanent detention, he'd have it, and there were all these rumors of sealed juvenile records and things like that.

And me, I was a kid who sometimes wore a basketball jersey to class. I was a sophomore with an outside shot at starting. In a year, I might be one of those guys who could go anywhere, talk to anyone. Or I might not. Like I said before, I didn't really hang out with a lot of other jocks. I doubt Krista, Elijah, or Les knew that, though. If you'd asked them four days ago who I was, they probably would've said, "That basketball player."

Now we were sitting here talking about everything except the noise we'd just heard, and it didn't seem like such an odd group anymore. Krista and I had talked a bunch of times now. And if she was more popular or thought she was better than us, she hadn't acted like it.

Elijah was actually pretty funny. He still didn't talk much, but he was always thinking, and I've got to say: What's so bad about that? And if he was a little negative about our chances in here, who's to say he wasn't right?

Les was the biggest surprise. He'd been fine. He was the first one of us to realize that Elijah wasn't the freak people said he was, and he really hadn't caused any trouble to anyone else. It was pretty clear to me now that it wasn't the other kids he had a problem with. It was the adults: all of the rules and late bells and all that crap.

I'd always sort of been afraid of him, because of his reputation and how he looked, but I'd never actually heard of him getting into a fight. He skipped class and broke things, and I was there when he showed up for gym in work boots. It was always things like that: one-fingered salutes to the school. I don't know what he had going on in his life that made him resent authority so much, but I knew that some people did. And I knew that it didn't really apply in here now.

As for me, I sort of wondered. If you asked these three about me now, what would they say? Would they say "He's friends with Jason and Pete" or "He's on my bus" or something like that? I was pretty sure it wouldn't be "He plays basketball." I'd settle for "He's OK."

I looked over at the window. Frost had formed along the edges and was sort of inching its way toward the middle.

"Earth to space cadet," someone said.

I turned back toward the group. It was Krista. She was looking right at me.

TWENTY-SEVEN

Maybe half an hour later, Pete and Julie came back with more food. Really, there wasn't a lot of variety to be found in the caf. They'd found rolls instead of bread, chocolate chip cookies instead of fake Oreos, strawberry jelly instead of grape. They did have one surprise though.

"Hot dogs!" said Pete, holding up a frozen block of plastic-wrapped wieners. "We can cook them right over the fire bucket."

Julie rooted through her backpack and produced a few forks. "We can use these as skewers," she said.

It was a little lame. I mean, what were we supposed to do, cook them one at a time while we were in there taking a dump? Still, it had been days since we'd had hot food, and just the idea of it was making my mouth water. You could see the dogs were still good. They were sealed in plastic and the ice was just beginning to drip off the corners. Truthfully, I wasn't even sure that kind of Grade D, every-preservative-known-to-man meat needed to be refrigerated. It wasn't that many steps up from a Slim Jim.

Anyway, the thought of cooked food was pretty exciting. Krista put her hands up in the air and shouted, "Cookout!"

I don't know if it was the noise or if it was just going to happen anyway, but right at that moment there was an enormous sound. It wasn't a slow rumble like before; it was a sharp, fast

BAM! like someone had fired a cannon thirty yards away. I closed my eyes and ducked my head, just out of pure instinct. As I did, I felt a shock wave shoot up through my feet. It felt like a one-second earthquake.

"What the−?" I said.

"Whoa!" said someone else, and a third person just screamed. I'd say it was one of the girls, but honestly, I think it might've been Pete.

I opened my eyes and got my bearings. The sound had come from out in the hallway. You know how you can just sort of tell which direction a sound is coming from? It was like that, but we felt it too. It had been so loud that we heard it in our ears and felt it in our bones.

We stampeded out into the hallway. I followed along, even though it seemed like maybe we were running the wrong way. Why run toward the disaster? As soon as I got out there, I could see that something was wrong.

At first, I thought that maybe the floor was tilted, but I looked down and it was fine. I looked back up and realized that it was the end of the hall that was out of whack. The line connecting the ceiling to the wall above the girls' bathroom was wrong. It was no longer level, no longer a neat horizontal line. Now the border between the ceiling and wall ran in a downward slope toward the back stairwell, as if the whole thing was getting ready to slide out of the building.

The door frame had been pushed out of shape beneath it. It had gone from a rectangle to a polygon and had knocked the door off its bottom hinge. The gap between the door and its frame had been filled by snow. There was a solid wall of snow behind the door and a tail of snow pushing into the hall.

I tried to process it all, standing there in the dim light. I was like a camera, developing a picture without understanding it. The image floated in my head like a dream. The angles were all wrong . . . and why was there snow in the hallway? None of it made any sense.

"What happened to the door?" said Les, his voice rising.

"Don't shout!" Elijah hissed in a loud whisper. And then I understood.

"The roof collapsed," I said, and that shut everyone up.

The roof had collapsed. Not all of it, or we would've been buried and crushed. But some of it had. The part over the far end of the second floor had come crashing down under the weight of the snow. I think the floor under it might've collapsed too. We were all in a little cluster in the middle of the hallway, looking at the damage.

I looked again at the little tendril of snow pushing out into the hallway. It looked like an animal to me, like something try-ing to get to us. If this had happened a few days ago, that snow would be starting to melt by now. But it had gotten so cold in here, the snow probably felt right at home.

I took a step back and looked straight up. Everyone else did the same. We craned our necks to look at the ceiling directly above us. It could just come down, right now, and squash us like half a dozen very cold bugs.

Jason came huffing back up the stairs. He'd heard the

collapse all the way down in the shop. He knew what it was immediately.

"This is not good," he said.

He said it quietly.

TWENTY-EIGHT

Jason took a few steps toward the end of the hallway, but that was as close as any of us were willing to go. After that, we went back to the room and began talking about it in quick, low voices.

"If it was because I shouted, why did it happen so far away?"

"Maybe we just got lucky."

"Yeah, for how long?"

No one had any answers, and eventually we got around to eating. I wasn't all that hungry, and I don't think anyone else was either. But there was a new batch of food in front of us, so we dug in. I even had seconds of the chocolate chip cookies. They were crumbly and cold but good. Right about then, it seemed like any meal could be our last.

Jason went across the hall to check on the fire bucket and came back chomping on a hot dog, no bun required. One and two at a time, we all did the same. I ate mine straight off the fork, and for the minute or so that I was chewing, I really did feel better. I guess it was a childhood thing. I used to eat hot dogs all the time back then.

But a hot dog apiece doesn't last long, and after we'd licked our fingers clean we were left sitting there in our little room again. The snow was coming down, the roof was coming down, it was all coming down. The whole time we'd been here, we'd thought: At least we've got this big, old school. When the snow buried the first floor, we moved to the second. When the heat and water went out, we built a little fire and melted snow.

But now, I mean, what could we do? This big, old school was a little too old and weak in the joints. We thought it would save us, but now it looked like it might be what killed us. I thought about the girls' bathroom, stuffed with sharp, busted wood and packed with snow. What if someone had been in there? Or what if it had been this room? Would have been crushed, frozen, suffocated? Whatever the flavor, we wouldn't be alive.

We'd turned the radio off to talk, but Pete turned it back on now. Andy hadn't been on all day. It was some new guy, and he didn't seem to know anything new or to play as much music. It still gave us something to listen to, something else to think about. But I couldn't help but notice that the light on the dial was almost out.

When Jason saw that he said, "Turn it off."

No one did, so he got up and did it himself.

"Well," he said, "now that I'm up." And he touched the tip of his hat and left the room.

"Where does he keep going?" said Julie.

It was up to me to explain his go-kart turned snow-kart, that it had been a shop project at first.

"You mean there are like motors and stuff here?"

"Yeah," said Les sarcastically. "It's called shop class."

"I know about that, but I thought you, like, read about that stuff in books. Like in the other classes. I didn't realize there were really tools in the school."

"Are you kidding me?" said Pete. "The school's full of 'em."

And that was a funny line, but no one laughed.

"Do you think it might really work?" Julie said to me after a few minutes of silence.

I hadn't really thought about it much. The radio had said to stay put, and that's what I'd assumed we'd do. Now, though, this didn't necessarily seem like the best place to be. One of the houses up on the slope seemed to be doing OK. It looked like maybe someone had been clearing snow away from the second floor windows, and there was smoke curling out of its chimney again. Maybe if we brought some food up there?

"I don't know," I said. "I guess it might. You definitely couldn't get more than one person on it, though."

Could it make seven trips, back and forth? Even one trip seemed to be pushing it.

"I'm going to go check it out," said Les.

After he left, it was quiet for a while. Pete got up to use the can in the bucket room, and right after he did, Julie left the room too.

"Uh, not my business," said Elijah, "but those two don't do *everything* together, do they?"

Krista and I laughed.

"That's nasty!" she said.

But when Pete came back, the first thing he said was, "Where's Jules?"

"We thought she was with you," said Elijah, and the rest of us snickered a bit.

"Seriously, where is she?" he said.

"I don't know," I said.

"Maybe she went to check out the snow thing," said Krista. It seemed like the most likely explanation. I mean, Krista still knew her best.

Pete stood by the door, looking out into the hallway. He was thinking about going after her.

"Geez, man, give her a break!" I said.

He looked over at me and laughed.

"Yeah, I guess there's such a thing as too much of a good thing," he said, puffing out his chest and fake flexing his muscles.

He sat down and for a while it wasn't so bad. Pete was talking about what he was going to do when this was all over, like how he was going to say he was "traumatized" and take a month off from school. "Just TV and video games," he was saying.

Pete talked really fast when he got excited, and he'd get excited over really dumb things. It was one of his best qualities. Everyone else tries to play it so cool all of the time.

Anyway, Pete was doing most of the talking, but we were chiming in with our own plans. When it was Elijah's turn to say what he was going to do, he shrugged and said, "Probably go back to the library."

We busted out laughing. He knew that's what we all used to think about him, that he was that weird kid in the library, and it was cool of him to bust on himself.

242

It was hard to stay in too good a mood in here, though. When I realized how loud I was laughing, I stopped mid-breath and looked up at the ceiling. Everyone else stopped too.

"Good one," I said after a moment.

TWENTY-NINE

Things were quiet for a while, and then we started rationalizing.

"There must've been a problem with the roof there," said Krista.

"Yeah," I said. "Could be. Maybe because of the pipes coming from the restroom and stuff. I mean, they could be frozen by now. Maybe they burst or something? You know how ice is bigger than water? That could've caused a problem."

"Wouldn't the pipes be under the floor, not over?" said Elijah.

"Not necessarily," I said. "You know in *Dirty Jobs* and *Verminators* and those type of shows, when they are always crawling around in attics or, like, above the ceiling panels in office buildings?"

"I know *Dirty Jobs*," said Pete.

"*Verminators* is kind of the same thing, but it's just about exterminators. Anyway, my point is, there are always a bunch of pipes and wires and stuff, and holes where all of that stuff goes between floors. That's usually where they set the traps."

"Yeah, so what are you saying, we have rats too?"

"No, no, just that there's probably all of that stuff here," I said. "And more because it's a bigger building. So there are some pipes that freeze and wires passing through holes in the floor, and it's all old and weak anyway."

"Your argument is old and weak," said Pete, smirking. "Probably do have rats, though."

"Whatever," I said. "I'm just saying it could've, like, contributed."

"Well, if it did," said Krista, "I mean, if that's what happened, will the boys' room be next?"

"Could be," I said. "Or maybe there just won't be another collapse. It could've been a freak thing."

"Yeah," said Krista. "It is pretty weird. If you think about it."

There really wasn't anything that weird about tons of snow busting through a worn-down, century-old roof. We were just trying to talk ourselves into it. There wasn't much else to do. We wanted to turn the radio back on, but with only four of us there, it seemed like a bad use of batteries. And, if I'm being honest, I sort of wished Pete and Elijah would leave the room for a while.

Nothing against those guys, I just wanted to be alone with Krista. We were already talking, and I knew I could keep it going if those two left. I thought I might even make a move, try to kiss her. I mean, what was I waiting for? I could die in here. We both could. I could be crushed or suffocated or frozen or D) all of the above, and it would happen fast. It's not like I'd get the chance to make a move if the roof came down.

But they didn't leave. I mean, where were they going to go? And it wasn't so bad, sitting there, talking about *Dirty Jobs* and whether or not the school had rats. And just as I was thinking about some of the craziest dirty jobs I'd seen, like "sewer inspector" and "leech trapper," Julie came bursting into the room. She was crying, really sobbing, and the front of her jacket was torn open. Little down feathers flew up when Krista ran over and grabbed her.

I looked over at Pete. His eyes were wide and he was sort of frozen for a second. Then he jumped out of his chair and his blanket fell to the floor. Elijah and I exchanged confused looks.

"Shhh, shhh, shhh," Krista was saying. "What happened? It's OK. What happened?" Then she hugged her again, and when she stepped back, Julie started talking.

Her words sounded small and quiet in between her sobs. I was looking at the tear in her jacket—Did that go all the way through? Was she injured?—and listening closely. I still couldn't make out most of what she was saying to Krista, but I did hear one word: "Les."

I guess Pete heard it too, because he took off. You idiot, I was thinking, and I meant both of them. I figured I'd been wrong about Les, but Pete was going to get himself beat down or worse. He couldn't take Les, no chance. It's like he'd just started running full speed toward a brick wall. I started after him. I wasn't sure if I was going to try to stop him or to back him up, but I knew I needed to catch him.

Krista grabbed me by the sleeve right before I reached the door. I started to shake her off and turned my head to tell her to let go.

"No," she said. "No."

THIRTY

"Not Les," she said. "Les."

At first, it made no sense to me. It was like listening to a baby babble. Then I figured it out: "Not Les," she was saying. "Less." As in less light than she thought, less heat, less air. Julie had gotten lost down there in the dark. She caught her jacket on something and got scared. Then things got worse, another wrong turn, maybe a trip or two, and she'd lost it. I thought the same thing was going to happen to me down there once or twice.

So I was putting this together in my head and then I remembered: Pete!

I took off out the door and along the hallway and started down the stairs. But you can't run in the dark. Or I guess you can, but it's not a good idea, and I wasn't going to be breaking up any fights with a broken leg.

I slowed down, but even then my mind was racing ahead. I took what I thought was the last step but there was one more. I stumbled forward and slammed my shoulder into the edge of the door frame. I swore loudly and heard it echo in the dark, empty hallway in front of me.

I made my way toward the shop at what I guess you'd call a brisk walk, definitely not quite a jog. I was feeling my way along the wall the whole time, smacking my fingers on locker handles and window frames. The nail of my middle finger caught in something and nearly pulled free. The pain was sharp and liquid and the darkness lit up with a pattern of white-yellow stars. I broke stride but then shifted over and started along the opposite wall using my other hand to guide me.

"Pete," I called out. "Don't! Stop!"

And that was stupid, because he could hear that and think: Pete, don't stop! Ambiguity was not my friend today.

"Pete," I tried again. "Don't do anything!"

That seemed clear enough. But I didn't hear anything. No response, no footsteps in front of me, nothing. It's kind of funny, because when Pete had taken the blanket and snuck away with Julie he'd used this trip as an excuse. He said he'd gotten lost on the way to the shop. I sort of hoped it was true this time, that he'd taken off like a rocket down the wrong hallway and right now he was wondering why there was a wall where there should've been a door. I hoped that was the case, but I sort of knew it wasn't.

I picked up my pace, as much as I thought I could. I really, truly did not want to lose another fingernail, though. My right hand throbbed and my left barely skimmed the wall. And, of course, I got there too late. Jason had to tell me later how it'd gone down.

Pete had thrown the door open, calling Les a son of a few different things, none of them good. He was yelling that Les had attacked Julie. *Molested* was the word he'd used, apparently, though I don't even know where he got that idea. Jealousy, possessiveness, whatever you want to call it, it can make guys pretty stupid.

254

Les said he hadn't done any such thing. That was good enough for Jason, because Les looked so genuinely surprised by the whole thing and had been in the shop for half an hour anyway. It wasn't good enough for Pete, though. He took the first swing, which I guess is how he landed it. Then Les had just dismantled him. He hurt practically every part of him. "It was like watching someone take apart a drum kit," Jason said.

Finally, Jason had been able to wade into all of the swinging limbs and pull Les off. Jason was a pretty tough kid himself, but what that really meant was that Les was ready to be pulled off.

By the time I got there, Pete was lying on his side on the floor, holding his hand up to his nose or his right eye or maybe both. Jason had Les in the opposite corner and was trying to calm him down.

"I know, man. I know," he was saying.

Then they all looked over at me: Jason over his shoulder, Pete out of his one good eye, and Les straight at me. I think maybe Les thought I was there to fight him too, because he took a step out into the open floor and you could see his shoulders were tensed up.

"No," I said, and put both my hands up. "No, no, no."

Then I knelt down next to Pete. I was mad at him, but he was my friend and he looked horrible. I brought him some snow from outside the window, and as cold as it was in there, he still cupped it in his hands and put it right on his face. The blood seeped in immediately, and after a few seconds it looked like he was holding a cherry snow cone.

Pete had thrown his gloves off at some point, and it took me forever to find the left one. It was darker in the room today. The snow was finally climbing the back wall, painted against the glass by the wind and layering on. There were a lot of shadows and dark corners, and Jason didn't help me look for the glove because he didn't want to leave Les alone. It seemed like even as messed up as Pete was, he might say something to Les, and Les would start kicking him again.

Eventually, I found the glove and we got Les out of there. Then we spent half an hour cleaning Pete up and getting him ready to head back upstairs. It didn't seem like anything was broken, just very badly bruised and a little bloody here and there. The mood lightened once we knew everything still worked, so I spent thirty seconds or so explaining to Pete the mistake he'd just made. Ambiguity was no friend of his either.

"Less," I said, "as in, You have less blood than you used to."

"As in, I look less pretty," he said, but it hurt him too much to laugh.

THIRTY-ONE

Things were bad after the fight. There was no option but to stay in the same room. With all of us in there, it could heat up by, like, ten degrees. Plus, that's where the radio and the food were, and the fire was right across the hall. We broke up into three groups, like we had in the beginning. The girls were in the back; Jason, Pete, and I were in the middle; and Elijah and Les were in the front near the door, as close to their old, abandoned room as they could get without being in the hallway.

We felt trapped in every way: in the school, in the room, in between the rising snow and the buckling roof. . . . It just didn't seem like we could last much longer like this.

Julie was quiet, except for her sneezes and coughs. Across the room, Pete was coughing and blowing his swollen nose now, too. In a weird way, it was almost like they were talking. But they weren't talking, not at all. Julie thought Pete was a violent jerk, a typical boy, whatever. She'd told him as much once things had settled down a bit. And Pete was too beaten down to try to talk himself out of the doghouse.

Every now and then, one of those two would get up to get another wad of toilet paper. Someone had put a roll on the windowsill, and it was the closest thing we had to Kleenex. But they never went up at the same time. Julie walked with an annoyed chop to her steps. Maybe she was embarrassed about getting lost and crying and being the cause of all this. Maybe she was embarrassed about the choice she'd made with Pete. Maybe she just thought we had enough problems without beating the crap out of each other, and she was right about that.

Whatever the case, she'd walk over to the sill in crisp, quick steps, tug some paper free, and wait till she was back in her seat to blow her nose. Pete would walk up there with a big limp on the right side and blow his nose on the way back. Les glared at him the whole way, a shiner forming around his left eye from the one clean punch Pete'd landed.

Jason and I weren't too happy with Pete either, but he was in bad shape. He was beaten up and sick and humiliated and it really didn't seem like we had any choice but to let it slide and sit with him. His stuff was right next to ours anyway.

We didn't talk to him much, though. We'd support him because he was our friend, but we'd do it more or less silently. Really, Les was the one who had the reason to be mad. Pete just assumed he'd, what, assaulted Julie? And then Pete had just run with it and gone after him, swinging. I sort of felt bad for Les. I would've felt worse for him if he hadn't completely demolished Pete.

We were all just sitting there, listening to the radio. None of us cared much about the batteries at the moment. Andy was back on and he started talking about rescue operations, about what the National Guard was planning if the storm stopped soon and what they were planning if it didn't. Everyone sort of perked up.

"Turn it up," said Krista, and I got up and did it.

But the announcement was over before I even got back to my chair. There really hadn't been much to it: "Hardest hit areas first" . . . focus on "at-risk populations" like the elderly . . . "single-story residences a priority."

We were trying to figure out what that meant for us and our families. Were teens an "at-risk population"? And that's when Les told the room what Elijah had told him, what Elijah had told me. That no one knew we were here.

I don't know why he did it. I think maybe he was just mad. Because Pete had just attacked him for no good reason, and now he was sitting with his friends in the center of the room. I'm sure it looked to Les like we were protecting Pete. I suppose we were, if it came to that.

Krista started crying and Jason got angry. He stood up fast and sent his chair skidding backwards across the floor. That was pretty much it, though. No one had the energy for another fight. Jason just said, "That's bull, my dad's not dead. He found some place to be." Then he went and got his chair and sat back down.

All the familiar thoughts bounced through my head, the ones I'd been picking at privately, like a scab. My mom was home. Her office would've sent everyone home early, and it was only like a mile from the house. The car could make it that far. Even if it only made it most of the way, what would that leave, like, a quarter mile? That's only once around the track. She could make that, so she was home. The house was a sturdy little block, and there was food there.

I'd run through these same calculations several times a day

since this had started. I'm pretty sure we all had, in some version or other. That was small picture, though. The big picture had shifted now. It sort of seemed more real now that everyone had heard.

All these days of waiting for someone to come and rescue us when maybe no one even knew we were here. Even after the storm stopped, how long would it take them to find us? We didn't know what was wrong with the phones or how long it would take to fix, but reopening the schools wouldn't exactly be priority number one. By the time they got to us, as likely as not, they'd be digging us out of the collapsed wreckage.

I didn't say it, but I didn't need to. Everyone was quiet, doing the math themselves.

Everyone was quiet, and I guess that's why we could hear the low whine above us. It wasn't a big rumble like before. It lasted maybe five seconds. It was a small, high-pitched whine, and it ended with a quick, sharp click. It sounded almost alive, though we knew it wasn't. It was something above us, some beam or brace. It was the sound of something giving up.

THIRTY-TWO

The day crawled by, and as early as it got dark, it still seemed sort of overdue. Over the last few days, we'd begun gathering around in one big group to eat our meals. Without anyone saying anything about it, that ended now. We sat there in our little groups eating in deep gray silence.

"It's slowing down," said Elijah, returning from the window.

And it was. It had been all day. No one had said anything about it because A) it had done this before, only to come back as strong as ever a few hours later, and B) it seemed like even one more flake could do it. Some tiny fraction of an ounce would turn out to be one tiny fraction of an ounce too many and it would all come down on us. Or it could stop dead, and the air could warm up, and the melting would trigger a collapse.

By nine o'clock, it was pitch-dark, inside and out, and we had no idea what the snow was doing. The radio still sounded OK, but the light behind the dial was gone, so we shut it off.

Nine o'clock, with no light and nothing to do. It was like being a little kid and being sent to bed at seven. It sucked. We all climbed under our blankets, though. At least I assume we all did. The only sounds were coughs and sneezes and noses blown in the dark.

By now, Jason and Krista had joined the sick list. I didn't think they'd be in the mood to pray, but I was wrong. I got out from under my blanket and, a few feet away, Jason did too. I started up, quieter now, really just murmuring, and I heard Krista making her way up to us.

I prayed to Gabriel again. I figured God and Jesus were hearing from a lot of people at this time of night. But who else was praying to the less glamorous of the two archangels, the one with the trumpet instead of the sword?

If I could've I would've asked him to put down that trumpet and pick up a snow shovel to clear off the roof for us but to step light when he did it. I didn't know a lot about angels, just what everyone knows plus what I'd learned the one year I went to Sunday school, but I knew they didn't do yard work. I prayed for him to keep my mom safe instead, though if I'm being honest, I was sort of hoping he'd be impressed by my selflessness. Another thing about angels, though, I'm pretty sure they don't fall for dumb tricks like that.

And then everyone was back under their blankets and there was nothing to do but wait for sleep. Is it better to die in your sleep? I stayed awake for hours and thought about that.

THIRTY-THREE

I don't know what time I got to sleep, maybe a little after midnight, but I know it was very early in the morning when the noise woke me up. For the record: Waking up in your high school on a Saturday sucks. I heard a sharp scratching sound and my eyes popped open instantly. The light in the room was still dim. The roof is coming down, I thought. This is it!

But it wasn't the roof. I got my bearings, adjusted a little, and I could tell that the sound wasn't coming from above me. It was coming from, where, beside me? I looked over. There was nothing there, just Pete's empty blanket and beyond that the door, slightly open. My brain worked slowly: The noise was coming from the hallway, and Pete wasn't in the room. . . . Pete was out in the hallway, making the noise.

The sound was getting closer, louder, and other people were starting to stir under their blankets now. I could've waited for Pete to make it to the room, since I was pretty sure that's where he was headed, but I climbed out from under my blanket and stood up. I was stiff and sore and could only imagine what Pete must've felt like: stiff and sore and bruised and clotted. But he was out there, dragging Lord knows what down the hallway.

On some level, I guess I did know what it was, because I remember thinking that I'd better get to him before Jason woke up. I moved as quietly as I could, and once I was out in the hallway, I closed the door behind me. Pete had left it open and our pathetic store of breath and body heat was escaping into the hall.

He was about halfway between the top of the stairwell and the room. The light was still dim outside and much dimmer in the hallway. Even at this short distance, Pete was just a shape dragging another shape. He was bent over at the waist and tugging the low, flat thing across the floor. It was Jason's snow-kart, of course.

As he got closer, I could see that his face was wet with sweat from the effort. The thing had no wheels now, just a tapered metal bottom like a large sled or a miniature boat. It moved like a stubborn animal, digging in and resisting every inch of the way. I'm sure it was leaving long scratches in the tile.

"I thought it would slide a little easier, you know?" he said when he got a little closer.

"Dude, man, what are you doing with it?" I said in a whisper.

"What do you think? I'm going to go for help, let them know we're here."

This raised a million questions. They flew up like sparks as my mind revved up, almost fully awake now. Where exactly do you plan to go? Is it gassed up? How do you know it even works? Who is "them"? But first things first: "It's not even yours."

"I helped build the stupid thing," he said. He was whispering now too. It was amazing how much whispering we'd done since we'd been here. Seven kids with the school to ourselves and still we felt we had to whisper.

"A little," I said. "Back when it was going to be a go-kart."

"Whatever," he said, but he stopped and stood up straight, as if he might be open to discussing the matter. While he waited, he wiped his forehead and face with the sleeve of his jacket. Nylon is not really an absorbent material, though, and he mostly just pushed the sweat across in long streaks.

I was selecting between the many counterarguments I could make when he got tired of waiting and said, "It's the reason I'm stuck in this dump."

"Maybe," I said, shrugging a little and giving him that one. We'd all stayed after to work on the thing. "But Jason's going to blow a fuse."

"Jason'll be fine."

"Did you even ask him?" I said, though it was pretty obvious he hadn't. Why else would he sneak down to get the thing at the break of dawn?

"Jason'll be fine," he repeated.

"I doubt it, that thing is, like—" I started, but Pete cut me off.

"Listen, man, I need to do this," he said, his voice finally rising above a whisper.

I looked at him now, really looked at him. My eyes had adjusted to the dim light out here and he was just a few feet from me. His face was covered in bruises, with visible swelling and burst blood vessels just beneath the skin. And it was more than just physical damage. You could see it in his expression: He was defeated, embarrassed.

It was bad enough to attack some guy for no reason, but it was worse to do it and lose so badly. It was bad enough to do it for a girl, but it was worse when she resented you for it. It was bad enough to ignore your friends for that girl for four days, but it was worse to go crawling back to them because you needed their protection.

"Yeah," I said, "maybe you do. But I don't know, man. Doesn't seem safe."

"Staying here doesn't seem all that safe either," he said. He was going to go on, but he had to stop to cough: three quick, hacking barks. When he did, his breath pushed out like tiny clouds in the dim light.

I'd gotten used to seeing everyone's breath when they talked, but this was different. It looked dangerous, pestilent. I could literally see where the germs were. They were hanging suspended in the spreading mist of his breath, and I stepped back to avoid them.

He went on: "Listen, it's letting up. They'll be out soon, looking for people, and they don't know we're here."

"We don't know that," I said.

"Makes sense to me."

Yeah, I thought, to me too.

"So I go out," he said, "find someone, anyone, maybe even a patrol, and let them know what's up. About the seven of us here, and the roof and all that. This stuff has got to be eighteen feet deep by now, still blowing and drifting like crazy. It's not like we can just march out into it once it stops. And when it starts to melt, it will shift, get denser. The water will find its way in, and then the whole thing'll come down."

He'd thought it through, I had to give him that.

"So what are you going to . . ." I said, finishing the sentence by gesturing toward the snow-kart.

"Gonna launch it out the window. It's only a few feet down to the snow now."

"You are one crazy dude," I said finally. My mind was flying now, considering the plan from different angles, and that was the only thing I could think to say.

"I need to do this, man," he repeated.

And he did. He needed to do something right. "Yeah," I said, "OK."

"Well, pick up the other end," he said. "This thing makes a racket on the floor."

I swung around and picked up the back end, because it got me away from the germ clouds of his coughing.

THIRTY-FOUR

So I was on board, but Jason still needed convincing. He was already sitting up in his chair waiting for us when we pushed our way in the door. His thick, dark fire blanket was draped over his lap, and his look was somewhere between annoyance and anger.

Everyone was up now. How could they not be with the entrance we made? We banged the thing against one side of the door frame and then the other, turned it sideways and tried again. We were huffing and puffing and swearing under our breath the whole time.

The kart was about the size of a bumper car, with a flatter bottom and a more skeletal frame. It was lighter than you might think, made mostly of metal pipes, curved aluminum, and a riding-mower engine. But it was unbalanced and awkward to carry.

The argument started as soon as we put it down.

"Do enough damage to it?" Jason said, and I realized that he thought I was in on the whole thing. He had no way of knowing that I'd just found out about it myself, out in the hallway not five minutes ago.

"Hey," I said. "I'm just helping him get it into the room. I told him he'd have to work it out with you."

That was sort of true. Jason thought it over for a few moments and then turned to focus on Pete.

Pete basically told him what he told me, without all the I-need-this stuff. He laid out the argument for going, but it still didn't explain why he was the one who should go or what right he had to take the kart. Jason pointed that out.

The rest of us mostly just listened to the argument. Our expressions shifted between skeptical and convinced, annoyed and sympathetic, depending on what point was being made and who was making it, but we let Pete and Jason settle it.

"Come on, man, I built the thing while you were up here playing video games and trying to hook up," said Jason, his eyes flicking over to Julie. That hit a little too close to home and pretty soon Pete started shouting. Before we could step in, Jason shouted back, and just like that: *GRRRRRRRRRMMMM!* The roof. It was no little whine and click this time. It was a big sound like the ones we'd heard before the first collapse.

Everyone froze for a second. Jason stopped mid-sentence, and he and Pete stood across from each other, red in the face but silent.

I know the snow above us was probably responding to the noise or its own internal dynamics or just the passage of time. But what it really seemed like to me was that it was responding to our anger. It seemed like it was growing angrier too, and unlike us, it had the power to do something about it.

"OK, go," said Julie in an urgent, hissing whisper. "Go. Someone go and tell them we're here."

"I'll go," said Pete, mouthing the words more than speaking them.

"No," mouthed Jason, shaking his head so there'd be no confusion.

Neither of them moved for a few moments. It was a stalemate. It was no longer about whether to use the snow-kart but about who would do it.

It came down to this: Pete wanted to do it, but it wasn't his kart. Jason had built the kart, but he didn't really seem to want to do it. It just seemed like he didn't want Pete to.

"Come on, man," I said as loud as seemed safe. "He dragged the thing all the way up here on one good leg. Give him a shot."

Jason looked over at me. His expression was that mix of hurt and surprise that is reserved for the betrayed.

"Yeah," said Julie, "give him a shot."

She was throwing in with Pete again, after all. I saw a little spark flash in Pete's eyes. What was it: joy, hope, life?

"Yeah," said Les. "Let the idiot kill himself."

Jason looked shocked. He couldn't believe what was happening: The kart he'd spent so long building was being taken away from him. He looked around for someone to take his side but no one did.

THIRTY-FIVE

Let the record show: I cast the first vote for Pete. I did it because I thought Jason was being petty, like taking his ball and going home. I was wrong about Jason's motives, but it was settled now, and motives didn't seem to matter anymore. Now it was about logistics: getting the thing over to the windowsill, getting the window open wide enough, lowering it down to the snow.

It took forever, like, seriously, forever. It was mostly Pete, Les, and me lifting, with Jason giving directions. About the best thing you could say about Pete and Les's teamwork is that they weren't actively taking swings at each other, and Jason seemed to be punishing us with bad directions.

And it's not like it was an easy job anyway. It wasn't that big, but it was an awkward shape. It was made of metal, and some of the edges were still sharp, so you had to be careful where and how you held it. I found that out the hard way, when the edge of the sled cut a long slice in my jeans.

"Put it down, put it down," I said halfway to the window.

I looked down at a patch of skin on the middle of my right thigh that my jeans used to cover. A thin red line of blood appeared like a slow smile.

"You ever think of sanding this down, man?" I said to Jason.

"It was on my list," he said. "Did I ever say it was finished? Before you frickin' hijacked it?"

Note to self: Do not complain to Jason about state of the kart.

Once we got it over to the sill, we realized that the bottom of the kart was wider than the windows. We had to set the thing down on the floor again and figure it out. We had to turn it, obviously, but we couldn't really hold on to the bottom edge to do it, not without cutting up our gloves and hands.

The wall had two big windows. We opened one, just so we could hoist the nose of the kart through and start rotating it. The windows opened upward and faced the exposed front of the building. As soon as we opened the window the three feet or so that we'd need to get the thing through, the wind blasted in like it had been waiting for us.

One thing was clear: The snow might have died down, but the wind was still going full strength. The force and cold were shocking and we quickly scrambled to close the window. Then we spent some time talking it out, so that when we opened the window again, we could get it through quick and get it closed. The fact that we were going to be throwing Pete out there, too, wasn't mentioned.

The talk was like, "OK, if you hold it here and I hold it there, then we can go, like, sort of three-quarters, right? See what I mean?"

"No, no, no. I'll hold it up by the nose and you two get it back by the engine," and round and round it went.

Pretty soon, it wasn't so early anymore. We were all hungry and the roof hadn't made any noise for a while, so it seemed like we might as well stop and eat something. Again, not mentioned, but that seemed especially true for Pete. We couldn't send him out into all that wind and cold and snow without, you know, some crappy pudding.

So we ate and listened to the radio on low volume, just in case there was some news that would make all this unnecessary. There wasn't: Rescue operations were still going to start with at-risk populations, and we still didn't know if anyone realized there was a population at the high school at all, much less how at-risk we were. It's not like Andy came on and said, "Hang in there, Tattawa, we're comin'!"

He just said the same things as before and got the Led out. It doesn't make much sense to play Led Zeppelin on low volume, but we left it on anyway. It was that Viking song, and it seemed appropriate: "We come from the land of the ice and snow..." Two minutes later, we were back at the window, lifting the kart up different ways, trying to eyeball what would work best.

"I'm not sure about this thing," Jason said. He'd said it a few times that morning, but I just thought he was fishing for compliments. The kart actually looked pretty slick. Krista and Julie hadn't seen the thing before, and they were all like, "This thing is cool!" and "How fast do you think it'll go?"

Elijah hadn't seen it before, either, and he signaled his approval simply by not saying anything morbid or overly apocalyptic about the idea. Basically, we ignored Jason's protests and a little before noon, the *Flammenwerfer* was sticking nose-first into the snow beneath the window. The extra heat we'd spent days building up in the main room had flown out the window with it, and Pete was preparing to follow.

This guy I'd known since he was literally not even four feet tall retied his boots and adjusted a pair of safety glasses he'd taken from the shop to use as ski goggles.

"What could possibly go wrong?" he said once he had them on securely. It was a joke, but none of us were in the mood to laugh.

He turned to Julie, said something that I'm sure he'd spent a lot of time thinking about but that none of us could understand. The fear was setting in, I guess, and before it dug too deep, he swung up onto the windowsill, took one last look back at us, and was gone.

We ran over and looked and he was past his waist in snow. I think he might've gone all the way down over his head, except that he'd grabbed the kart and was holding on to the side like a swimmer at a raft.

As soon as he hauled himself most of the way up onto the thing, we closed the window. That probably sounds bad, but then you're probably sitting in a warm room somewhere, not standing there with the freezing wind blasting the feeling right out of your face and knocking things over in the room behind you.

So yeah, we closed it and went right back to hoarding our body heat in that little box. Every heartbeat and every cloud of fog from every dumb thing we said made the room just a tiny bit less cold than it had been the moment before. Which meant that nothing we said could be all that dumb. We were literally saving our breath.

We watched Pete through the glass. He was bundled up as round and plump as a ripe berry, layered with anything he'd been able to borrow or trade for. He had Julie's scarf over his own and my sweatshirt over his own and under his jacket. He had a pair of work gloves on top of his ski gloves, and a pair of gym socks over his regular socks and under Jason's boots, which he'd exchanged for his own.

Jason had given him his cell phone too, which was pretty big of him, all things considered. "Try it once you get out there a ways," he'd said. "You know how it is around here with all these hills."

Pete had nodded, but he'd barely managed to stuff the thing in a side pocket with both pairs of gloves on. Now that he was out in the snow, his movements were even slower and clumsier underneath all those layers. He moved like a bundled-up baby. When he dragged himself up and into the little driver's seat, it looked like the whole thing might tip over and deposit him back in the snow. But the kart had settled on its boatlike bottom and it was just stable enough.

He brushed some of the snow off his jacket and legs and turned around and gave us a thumbs-up. The guys gave him a thumbs-up back and the girls clapped. Then he went to work trying to start the engine with the pull cord. Four good tugs and nothing. I was about to ask Jason if there was gas in there, but the thing sputtered to life on the fifth pull.

Pete turned and faced forward in his seat, grabbed on to the wheel, and prepared for the rocket start. The propeller was a gray metal blur, kicking up snow, but the kart just sat there for a while. It was dug into the snow but after maybe twenty seconds, with Pete leaning forward and making little scooting motions in the driver's seat, it began to pull free. It moved a few inches at a time at first, but then it began to slide along its aluminum belly: slowly, slowly, and then a little faster.

I looked over at Jason with my hand up for a high five, but he left me hanging. There was more clapping around us now. "Go, Pete, go!" someone said. But Jason wouldn't take his eyes off his little shop project, five yards away, then ten, then fifteen.

It was all planned out. Pete was headed to the center of town: the post office, the town hall, and the handful of stores that made up the wildly unimpressive downtown district of Little River. If it didn't look like he was going to make it that far, he was supposed to go to the little power substation. It seemed like that would be a priority for them. And if it didn't seem like he'd make it even that far, well, anywhere with people, anywhere other than this dead-end road in the middle of nowhere would do.

For now, he was headed northeast, toward the center of town. It seemed like a good start, and the kart was picking up speed now. The airboat design worked well on the snow, with the big propeller pushing the flat metal bottom along the surface. I looked back at Jason because, I mean, he had to be at least a little happy about that, even if it was someone else driving it.

He looked back at me and just shook his head: No. That's when I knew. It hadn't been pettiness that had made him try to stop Pete from taking the kart. He'd been trying to save him.

I looked back, squinting through the lightly falling snow and trying to see what was wrong, why Jason was wearing that hangdog look. At first, I thought he might be wrong about it. Or I guess maybe *hoped* is a better word.

Pete was halfway across the Great Lawn, three quarters, almost to the road! He was making fast progress, clipping along, but something else was happening too. Now I saw it. The nose of the kart was riding lower than the rear.

"I had the weight wrong, the balance," said Jason, almost to himself.

The pointed nose was digging into the snow, casting a little wake of white flakes off on either side. It was sinking in deeper as it went, maybe an inch down for every twenty yards forward. And then, at the edge of the road, it just went too deep. The point of the nose dug in and stopped, but the propeller kept going, pushing the back end up and over.

The snow-kart flipped; it happened fast. One second, we were watching Pete, hunched into the seat and leaning forward into the wind. The next, he was gone and all we could see was the shiny metal bottom of the kart, snow-scrubbed and sticking up toward the sky.

The propeller dug into the snow and ground to a stop. A few seconds later, thick black smoke started coming up from under the kart. We all shouted at the same time, some with words, some just screams. We forgot about the roof for a moment.

"No no no!" I shouted. "Pete! PETE!"

The smoke was coming up from underneath the flipped kart; underneath, where Pete was; where he must have been, though we could no longer see him.

THIRTY-SIX

Nothing moved except the drifting smoke and the falling snow. The kart was motionless, a little silver lump capsized on top of eighteen feet of snow. Even though it was maybe two hundred yards away, it seemed impossibly remote, as if we were watching it on television. I stared at it through the glass.

He was under there, in the snow and the smoke: Pete, my friend since forever. We had to get him out, but it seemed impossible. How could we close that distance? Pete hadn't made it even one foot without the help of the kart.

There was shouting and swearing all around me. Then, in a little gap in the noise, I heard someone say, "The roof." It was like hitting the mute button. In the sudden silence, I remembered something. I had my own project, something that might help, my Occam's racers. But they were down in the shop and not even finished.

"I have to go," I said. No one paid much attention.

Jason was wrestling the window open as I turned to head out of the room. The last thing I heard before I closed the door behind me was the howling of the wind and Jason yelling, "Pete! Pete!"

I thought maybe that was OK, since he was leaning out of the building to yell. There was no chance Pete would hear him, though. We would have to get closer, and we had no way to do that, so right now it was up to him. He would have to crawl out from under there. I could picture it, him climbing out from under there like a bug, tipping the thing back over, and climbing back on.

Maybe he could get that thing going again. It still had half a propeller. That wouldn't be enough to get him to town, but it might be enough to get him back to us. Or maybe he could just sit tight and bundled up long enough for me to get to him.

First, I had to get to the shop. I ran to the end of the hallway and took the turn down the stairs fast, but then I descended into that familiar, frustrating darkness. The nail of my middle finger had turned purple underneath, almost black with dried blood. It felt loose. It would fall off soon.

But, I mean, what was one fingernail? Or ten? What was a finger, for that matter? Pete was wedged upside down in the snow, and if he didn't freeze to death, that black smoke could turn into flame at any moment. Maybe it already had. Where there's smoke there's fire, right?

So, what I'm saying is, I went as fast as I could. And, yes, I'd made the trip a bunch of times now, but the trip is different at different speeds. Five steps before the turn becomes three or four if you're running. The middle of the hall becomes your face smashed into a locker. I took my lumps but I got there fast.

The shop was really dark now. I went over and slammed the windows open and closed to get more light in. That trick wouldn't work much longer. Even at the edge of the slope, the snow was climbing the building now. I slammed the windows hard. I think I heard a pane break somewhere, but I got enough light to work by.

Snowshoes, how hard could they be, right? I had the frames and the bottoms pretty well attached. I was using canvas. All the ones I could remember from books and movies and stuff were made of webbing, like oversized tennis rackets. But the idea was to spread out your weight over as much area as possible, right? So I figured something solid and light made just as much sense. Plus, webbing would've taken longer, and there was a roll of tan canvas right in the corner.

I still had to figure out some way to keep my feet in the things. I'd been leaving that for last because, well, why not? I was just making these things to stay busy, to have a reason to hang out with Jason. But now I needed them, and fast.

My first thought was duct tape, the first answer to every quick fix, but that was a bad idea. It would come off in the snow and I'd be stuck halfway across the Great Lawn with two big useless donkey paddles. I snagged the straps that Jason had been planning to use for a seat belt, and I got to work.

It was taking too long: the trip here, the windows, the scrounging, the cutting, everything. How long could a person survive upside down in the snow: minutes, hours? I didn't know. It didn't feel like I had a choice. These things needed to stay on my feet, or I'd be stuck out there too. I cut and fit the straps, drilled some holes in the metal frames, and connected it all up. The whole thing took maybe an hour.

I put them on and took a half dozen steps across the room. I was walking like a duck, making *FWOP-FWOP-FWOP* sounds as

I went, but it seemed to work. I took them off, put them under my arm, and banged and bumped my way back upstairs.

Smoke stung my eyes as I opened the door to the main room. They'd brought the fire bucket in from across the hall. The room was hazy and stunk of burning textbook. I heard a few coughs, but I couldn't tell if they were from the smoke or the cold bug that almost everyone had now.

"Just for a while," said Krista. "It was so cold in here."

I didn't care about the smoke. I was about to have all the fresh air I could stand, maybe more.

"Anything?" I said.

"No," said Jason. "It sort of shifted a little a few minutes ago, but I think that was the wind."

The window was closed again. Out on the snow, the kart was still upside down but it was tilted a little more to the side now. I still couldn't see anything underneath.

"You going out there in those?" said Les.

"Yep," I said.

I thought they might try to stop me: "No, Scotty, you can't! Don't be a fool!" But we couldn't just leave Pete out there, and everyone could understand snowshoes. This wasn't some crazy shop experiment. So instead of arguing, they just started handing me extra things to wear. There wasn't much left after Pete, but I ended up with a second hat and a pair of gym shorts over my pants. Jason traded me Pete's boots for my cruddy, funkified sneakers, and I tied my blanket around my neck like a cape.

I caught my reflection in the window, right before Jason and Les opened it. I looked like some sort of cut-rate superhero. We opened the window one more time. I climbed up and sat on the windowsill, and Krista handed me the snowshoes, first the right and then the left.

If this was a movie, this is the point where Krista would've leaned over and kissed me. "For luck," she would've said, like Princess Leia in *Star Wars*. But she didn't. I think you've figured out by now that this isn't about boy-gets-girl. It's about survival. She didn't even look me in the eyes when she handed me the shoes. I didn't take it personally. I think she probably just thought enough people had died in the snow.

I leaned out into the open air and fastened the shoes tight, and then there was nothing left to do but go. Anything I said would've sounded like last words, and I certainly wasn't going to turn around and give them all a thumbs-up.

I hopped down onto the snow, concentrating on getting both snowshoes to land at the same time and on the same level. Maximum surface area, that was the key. I counted in my head: 1-2-3. And then I went.

THIRTY-SEVEN

The wind whipped snow into my face. A large flake stuck on one of my eyelashes and I brushed it away with the back of my sleeve. I immediately regretted not taking a pair of safety goggles, like Pete had. Could I go back for them? Just as the thought crossed my mind, I heard the window slam behind me.

Forward, I thought. Move forward. I went to pick up my right foot, and that's when I discovered my second mistake. The canvas didn't want to come free from the snow. I'd wanted surface area to stay on top of the soft snow, but I'd gotten too much. The canvas was clinging to the snow and vice versa. So *that's* why they used webbing for snowshoes. I hadn't really gotten that before.

I had to reach down and tug my right foot free with my arms. I did the same with my left, but it got easier after that. I'd sunk a few inches in after the little hop from the window, but as long as I stayed on the top of the snow and kept moving, I didn't need my arms to pull free.

It was slow going, though, leaning forward into the wind and flapping these big canvas paddles under me. If I had to compare it to anything, I'd compare it to walking in deep mud. By the time I made it fifteen yards, my head was sweating underneath my two wool hats, and my face and thighs were almost numb with cold. I say almost numb because I have to account for the sharp, pricking pain that I felt with each strong gust.

After thirty yards, the cold was creeping inside my ski gloves. I flexed my fingers, balled them up, flexed them again. They wanted to go numb, but I was going to need them when I reached the kart. And I just tried to keep on like that, moving forward and making little adjustments as I went, in a long, head-down slog across the Great Lawn.

Somewhere under all this snow there was a statue. It was a statue of an oak tree: How dumb is that? Why not just plant an oak tree? You couldn't see it now, but I aimed for where I thought it was and I think I passed right over it. Five or six feet down: a fake frozen tree.

And then I was past it and I picked another target: the spot where some seniors had carved donuts into the grass with their cars a few months back. I know the shortest distance is a straight line, but I wasn't going very far out of my way. Instead of one straight line, I'd make the trip in two or three. I was just giving myself something to think about, and it helped not to be directly sideways to the wind.

Eighteen feet above the torn-up grass, I finally turned to face the kart. I think I'd been afraid of what I might see as I got closer, but it didn't really make sense to head anywhere else at that point. I had maybe thirty yards to go, and I just went ahead and did it, one floppy canvas clown foot in front of the other.

It was hard work lifting them. Not only did the canvas bottoms cling to the snow, but the snow kept building up on top of them. Webbing would've let the snow fall right through. Why, after thousands of years of the same basic design, had I thought I could build a better snowshoe? The snow on top of mine added another pound or two to each step, and if that doesn't sound like a lot, all I can say is you weren't out there.

My quads and calves ached, and the cold was no relief. It didn't cool my engines when the wind cut through the denim of my jeans, it just added another ache on top, another burn. Again and again, the cold wind found its way inside of the little cut the kart had made in my jeans.

My eyes were watering with wind and pain and frustration when I saw the kart. It was maybe ten yards away, just close enough to see with my head bent down and my chin tucked into my neck. The image of its bright silver bottom was broken up and refracted by my watering eyes. I sucked down a dose of snot, wiped my eyes, and, best I could, started running.

"Pete!" I shouted. "Hey, Pete!"

I'd had to pace myself to get there. There was no way I could've run even a quarter of the distance. Even shouting seemed like too much energy to spend. I'd kept the destination in mind and just slogged it out. But now that I was almost there, I let myself remember why I'd come.

"You dug in under there?" I said. I guess I was sort of hoping he was using the kart for shelter. Maybe he was even under there trying to fix it.

"Pete!" I shouted again.

Now I was kind of mad that he wasn't acknowledging me. My quads burning, my calves aching, and my eyes watering, I reached out with both hands. I wanted him to see me, to know that I was there, and so I pushed over his shelter.

Except that it wasn't his shelter; he was long past that. The kart fell the rest of the way over onto its side with a slow, heavy thud, and I saw him there.

I don't know what you want me to say here. I think you know what I found. He hadn't built a shelter. He wasn't down there working on the engine. He'd knocked himself out in the crash and died in the snow.

For a second, I saw it all: the soft horrible blue that had crept into his face, the way his hands were frozen stiff, like the curled talons of a bird.

I could go on; I remember every detail. But I won't. That's all you need to know. It's not something you ever want to see.

I turned around toward the school. I knew they were all watching through the window. I even saw a few faces, just little circles hovering behind the glass. I tried to fall down into the snow. The bindings at my ankles would only let me fall sideways, so that's where I went. My shoulder dug in deep and I felt the snow against the side of my face.

I guess I just leave him here, I thought. If he was alive, I could've helped him. But he wasn't, and I sure couldn't carry him. It was hard enough moving myself in these crappy snowshoes.

Hard enough moving myself...I turned that over in my mind. Man, it would be hard enough just getting back up again. I'd spent all of my energy getting here and making that stupid sprint at the end. I had no idea what came next. A deep shiver went through me, and I realized just how cold I was. It wasn't just my hands anymore, not just my feet and arms and legs and face. I was cold inside, in my chest, my back, everywhere.

I knew how it worked: Your body temperature drops, not even that much, like twelve degrees or something. Then you go to sleep. Then you die. It didn't seem like that bad a deal.

You might think I was delusional or something, but I wasn't. I was the opposite. Everything seemed really clear to me at that moment. I had three choices: I could turn around and go back to the room. It would be hard, but I thought maybe I could do it. I would sit by the fire bucket and get the feeling back in my fingers and toes. It would be so painful to feel all of those pinpricks again, the same ones I'd had when the feeling left me.

And then I would just sit there and wait for the roof to come down or for someone to come find us, whichever came first. So that was option number one.

Option number two: I could go to sleep and die. It felt like I was already halfway there. I might even be kind of a hero. At least I tried, right? I was just done in by my lame snowshoes. It was a design flaw. I would be like Jason's dad and Gossell and who knows how many others. Wrong place, wrong time: See you in the spring.

And that brought me to option number three: I could get my lazy butt up and keep going. I couldn't make it to town, but the power substation was half that distance. I still didn't think I could make it, but if I was honest with myself, I didn't know that I couldn't. And now—lying in the snow and going numb—seemed like a good time to be honest with myself.

It's funny. You'd think that if I imagined anyone's voice in my head right then it would've been my mom or maybe one of my friends. But it wasn't. It was my basketball coach, Coach Kielty, the guy with one-and-a-half eyes on me at practice all the time, the guy who'd taken a gangly underclassman and made him into a real athlete. And, more to the point, the guy who'd made me run all those stairs and laps.

"I got us a new StairMaster machine," he'd say. "It's at the top of the stairs. Go get it!" Or sometimes: "The point is not to see who can shuffle the fastest; the point is to pick up your feet!" Or just: "Go, go, go!"

I think he thought he was yelling at a wall half the time, but I heard him. I still heard him. I remembered the time after I hit that late three-pointer against Hanging Rock: "You know, Weems, you might amount to something here."

I wouldn't amount to anything in the snow. And I didn't train all off-season to give up now. I pulled my legs up, rolled onto my side, and got up. I got up on my big canvas feet.

THIRTY-EIGHT

It was probably a little after three o'clock. The school was well behind me now, and I was pretty sure I'd made a mistake. There probably weren't even two more hours of daylight left. I wasn't sure I could make it to the substation by then, and I wasn't sure it would matter if I did. What if they weren't there, what if power wasn't a priority yet?

I started looking for other options. There weren't many houses this far from the center of town. To be honest, there weren't even that many in the center of town. There were some out here, though. I'd already passed a handful of them, but I hadn't seen any lights or any signs of movement. The first few had just been roofs, the sides barely poking out and the tops wearing heavy peaks of snow like hats. I didn't see how being in there would be any better than being back in the high school. And I really, really did not want to stumble across any more claw hands and blue faces.

I kept going. Had everyone gone into town? Maybe to the town hall, where the fallout shelter was? I used the tops of telephone poles as guides and stayed over the road. The houses would be along the side of it, and this was the route the National Guard would take.

There was a little fork in the road a quarter mile ahead, where Route 7 met River Road. I looked up and there was something moving. It was a little figure, a man, scissoring his legs back and forth. He was skiing. I blinked into the wind and wiped the snow from my lashes. I saw the thin, red cross-country skis gliding underneath him and his black ski poles stabbing the snow. He was following the turn of River Road, heading toward Route 7.

I called out, but he was upwind and too far away. I kept my eyes trained on him. He turned his head my way at the intersection. It was habit I guess, checking to see if anything was coming. It seemed kind of funny under the circumstances. I felt like saying, "There's nothing coming, dude. You're clear for about three states."

I think he must've seen me when he looked back. There wasn't much else out here, and I wasn't exactly going to sneak up on anyone. I was moving in big exaggerated steps, with my arms out for balance and my blanket flapping around behind me. But if he saw me, he didn't let on. He paused for a second or two at the intersection and then moved on.

I set a slow course to intercept him, or his tracks, anyway. We were headed in the same direction now, but he was moving much faster than me. That wasn't saying much, of course. He was moving across the snow in smooth, even strides, while I was stomping across it like I was mashing potatoes with my feet.

And the potatoes were winning. I was seriously broken down at this point. I was operating in a zone past fatigue. I was just a numb engine chugging slowly along, trying not to think about what I'd seen. My brain sent signals to my legs and, for now, my legs responded. The less I thought about it, the better. If I really thought about it, about how tired I was and how much energy it took to keep going, I was pretty sure I'd stop. I had no feeling at all in my hands or my face.

The skier's movements were so sleek and effortless that it was like he was mocking me. I must've looked like Frankenstein's monster out here.

At first, I'd been happy to see someone else, another human being. But when he didn't stop for me, I started to get angry. Now I was getting angrier with every step. I was mad at him for moving better than me, for being farther ahead, for having enough feeling in his hands to use his ski poles.

It wasn't his fault, of course. I hadn't made skis because they didn't seem like a good bet in the really driving, heavy snow. It seemed like they'd bog down, get stuck. So instead I made snowshoes that bogged down and got stuck even in light snow. I couldn't exactly blame him for that.

This guy had just waited for the heaviest snow to stop and then taken out his skis. How many others had done the same thing? Now he was moving easily over the snow, putting another forty yards between us since the last time I looked.

"Where's the fire, jerk," I said under my breath. But I knew, just like he did. At any moment, the really heavy snow could start falling again. The storm had done that before. It had taken a break only to come back as strong as ever. We could be in a whiteout, or it could be hail, or freezing rain, or the wind could kick up a few more notches. I took some weird satisfaction in the thought that, if any of those things happened, we'd both be dead.

I remember thinking this: With my last breath I'd take his fancy skis and make a cross over his body. Here lies a man who thought he was hot stuff. I'm not proud of that, but you get mean pushing yourself past exhaustion in the freezing cold on the day your friend died.

I'm not sure why I kept following him, even when he was barely a dot in the distance, even when it was clear that he wasn't peeling off to go to the substation, that he was going on into town. Even when it was getting dark, and my body could only give me one or two steps a minute.

Part of it was that I figured he knew where he was going. A man doesn't go that fast without a pretty good idea of his destination. And part of it was that I did not want to be beaten by a guy in a bright blue ski suit. The rest of it, I don't know. I think maybe I wanted to go all the way into town because that's where Pete had been headed, and Pete wouldn't ever get there.

I kept going. Even when I couldn't see the skier ahead of me on the road anymore, I kept going, taking a step when I could. I was down to maybe a step a minute.

Finally, when I couldn't even see his tracks in the darkness, I stopped. Standing there, ready to topple over, I caught a whiff of wood smoke. Somewhere nearby there was a house with a fireplace and people. I needed to get there, but it was too late. My legs had stopped, and they were not going to start again.

I was standing, and then I wasn't. My eyes were open, and then they weren't. I was conscious, and then I wasn't. I was out cold.

THIRTY-NINE

I heard something. Lying there in the snow in something deeper than sleep, there was a sound loud enough to bring me back to the surface. Lying there with eyes that barely worked, there was a light bright enough for me to see it. I knew what it was: It was an angel, come for me at the end. I was ready, and it was my time.

FORTY

As the angel descended to collect me, to welcome me or dismiss me, to do whatever it is they do with the dead, I could hear his wings. The air beat the snow beneath me. It sounded familiar. I tried to remember. My brain wanted to run back over my whole life, to show me everything, but I made it stop and pause on one thing.

The air beat the snow beneath me. The sound was strangely familiar.

FORTY-ONE

The angel lifted me up and carried me away. And there was more than one angel now. My eyes were not working well in the dimness, but I could hear them. I listened to them talk. There were two voices, then three, and I wondered which one was Gabriel.

"Weak but stable, hypothermic," one of them was saying.

I was hearing OK but having trouble processing the words. Then I felt something: a rough tug on my arm and then a quick flash of pain. A warm sensation began to wash through me.

After that, things started to come back into focus and the words started to make more sense. I raised my head, just a little, and turned it to the side. I was inside a little cabin. There were three people with me, two men and a woman, all wearing helmets and uniforms. There was a constant rhythmic beating in the air all around me: *FWOOP FWOOP FWOOP.* I was in a helicopter.

I turned my head one more tick to the side and realized the closest man was looking right at me. "Hey," one of us said. I was pretty woozy, but I think it was him.

"Hey," he said, or I repeated.

"How you feeling?" And that was definitely him.

"OK," I said. "Better. Alive."

"Yeah, you're talking," he said. "That's a good sign, lifewise."

I looked around again. The other two people seemed to be

very busy. I couldn't make out what they were doing, but their uniforms were green.

"Are you the Army?" I said.

"National Guard," the man said.

"Massachusetts?" I said. "Connecticut?"

"Tennessee," he said.

"Huh."

"The Volunteer State," he said, and now I noticed a slight accent.

I didn't know what to say, so I just told him the truth: "I thought you were an angel."

"Heck, kid," he said, smiling. "I'm not even an officer."

"Sergeant Marten," he continued, "and who might you be?"

"Scotty," I said. "Scotty Weems. I don't have a rank."

He thought that last part was funny, but I didn't mean it as a joke. Things were still kind of foggy for me. I tried to sit up, but that wasn't happening. I felt a tug on my arm, and I looked over and saw that there was an IV hooked up to it. That made sense. I looked at the spot where the needle disappeared under a wad of gauze and tape.

"So where you coming from?" the sergeant asked.

And then it all came rushing back, and I started talking, too fast and all at once.

"Whoa, whoa, whoa!" he said. "Come again?"

"The high school," I said. "Tattawa. It's just . . . close. It's close to here."

I realized I didn't know how long we'd been flying or in what direction. Sergeant Marten reached up to his face. He had a small mouthpiece coming from his helmet. He covered it with one hand and said a few words, but between his hand and the rotors, I couldn't make them out.

"Roger," someone called back from farther up. "I got it."

I tilted my chin forward and my head followed. I saw another person, all the way at the front. It was the pilot, outlined against a bank of glowing instrument panels.

"There anyone there with you?" said Sergeant Marten. "A teacher or someone?"

"No teachers, but there were seven of us there," I said. It didn't seem like I had time to tell him about Gossell right now. I'd do that next.

"So there are, uh, six students still there?"

"Five," I said.

"I thought you just said . . ." he began, and then he got it. "Oh. OK. Roger."

He put his hand to his mouth again and began speaking, faster this time. I still couldn't hear him when he talked like that, and it was frustrating.

"They need help," I said. "It's bad."

"Yeah," he said. "High school sucks."

I heard one of the others laugh behind him, just one loud "Heh!"

"I'm serious," I said.

"I know it," he said, and I felt the floor shift beneath me, the helicopter banking hard left, heading back the way we'd come. It was like the world had tilted sideways on its axis. It had been doing that a lot lately.

ABOUT THE AUTHOR

ABOUT THE AUTHOR

Michael Northrop has written short fiction for *Weird Tales*, the *Notre Dame Review*, and *McSweeney's*. His first novel, *Gentlemen*, was published to starred reviews and named an ALA Best Book for Young Adults. It also earned him a *Publishers Weekly* Flying Start citation for a notable debut. An editor at *Sports Illustrated KIDS* for many years, Michael now writes full-time from his home in New York City.

Visit him online at www.michaelnorthrop.net.